LOVING
—FROM A—
DISTANCE

BETTY WILSON

WESTBOW
PRESS®
A DIVISION OF THOMAS NELSON
& ZONDERVAN

WestBow Press books may be ordered through booksellers or by contacting:

WestBow Press
A Division of Thomas Nelson & Zondervan
1663 Liberty Drive
Bloomington, IN 47403
www.westbowpress.com
844-714-3454

ISBN: 978-1-6642-0963-3 (sc)
ISBN: 978-1-6642-0950-3 (e)

Print information available on the last page.

WestBow Press rev. date: 12/21/2020

CHAPTER
ONE

Sitting alone on the porch swing day dreaming of the neighbor's grandson James Williams. Brenna Smaller is a eleven years old girl that is smitten with James the new neighbor's grandson. Brenna noticed him the day they moved on to the Woodland estates. George and Ella Smaller is Brenna's parents and they are neighbors of Jefferson and Claudia Summers.

James 13, and his two siblings Stephanie 17, and Rodney 20 are the kids of Kendra Summers Williams and James Kenneth. Johnny 14, and his two sisters Erin 17, and LaToya 19 are the kids of Kiera Summers Williams and Johnny Andrew. They are all the grandchildren of Jefferson and Claudia Summers. Their daughters married the Williams brothers, James Kenneth and Johnny Andrews Williams.

The Summer's Jefferson and Claudia had twin daughters, Kendra and Kiera that had been killed in an accident on their way back from dropping their children off to school. Their plans were to go to the mall on the way back from the school and then spend the rest of the day with the realtor, but a drunken driver cut their life short by hitting their car head on and the four of them were killed instantly. Their kids are now being raised by their Grandparents Jefferson and Claudia Summers.

Brenna and Julie are friends of the Williams and Brenna and Julie are only eleven years old while James is thirteen and Johnny fourteen. Brenna's parents George and Ella Smaller are old fashion parents with strict rules for all their children. They loved their kids and wanted to protect them from everything. The kids all worked very hard to stay on the honor roll. Brenna's parents are the greatest parents and they wanted their kids to have the best education to succeed in life. They are Christian people that kept their children in church every Sunday and they were in all activities at church. So, when Brenna went to church James was there as well. Both families just have a love for Christ Jesus. Brenna, James and Johnny sing in the choir together. The boys sang in the choir just to talk to Julie and Brenna. There were a lot of communication going on between James, Brenna, Julie and Johnny in the church. Brenna's mom and her dad would always have her get up and sing in church. Sometimes they would have her siblings Ivan, Kim, and Leah sing as well. Brenna use to hate this because she was so shy, but as she grew older and understood the love for Christ Jesus and how he died to save all mankind, she did not have a problem singing. She sang with her sisters and brother in a gospel group. Julie had learned to love singing and praising the Lord. James and Johnny's grandparents were Christians parents as well and kept them in church too. Julie's parents, were Daniel and Mary Glass. They were all neighbors and all had similar lives. Julie's parents went to a different church but soon joined the church where the Smaller's and the Summers were members of. Their denomination was Baptist/Protestant as well. They did not have to drive a distance anymore for church.

James, Julie and Brenna attended the same school together for one year and James moved on to junior high school with his cousin Johnny. Brenna never said too much when James was around, but she was always smiling at him and he would wink his eye and she would almost melt in her tracks. She was so cool with that because she knew she had his attention. Brenna was actually captivated with this young man. She knew she really liked him a lot even at this age but could not say anything to anyone about her feelings for this young man. She loved him from a distance.

Brenna and her girlfriend Julie would giggle all the time when they were around James and his cousin Johnny. Julie liked Johnny as well and they were silly eleven-year old's, with huge crushes on these young men. They always talked about how cute they were but they were too young to date or even talk to young men. This never kept Brenna from day dreaming about James. He would always smile at her and he treated her with the utmost respect. What she didn't know was her father William Smaller had seen them watching her and her friend Julie Glass and he told them we were too young and they were never to bother us unless they wanted to deal with him and Mr. Glass Julie's father. So, James backed off and would only smile at us and wink his eye when her father was not around. After all she was the neighbor's daughter and he would always watch out for her and her friend. He really liked Brenna very much but she was young and he was only thirteen himself and neither was old enough to date. James never mentions this to his cousin Johnny because he would tease him and he did not want to be teased about the girls.

Since attendance was low in all the churches each church would have a Sunday to worship and have Sunday school. Everyone went to a church and that was the way of life in the South. There were a few churches that had their own service every Sunday but they had enough members to carry their service. Brenna's church was the fourth Sunday and James and Johnny's church were the second Sunday. Julie's church was the third Sunday and the first Sunday was another church. So, they had time to see each other every Saturday and Sunday during the month without being in school. The Smaller's, Glasses and Summer's had all joined the same church so the kids could sing together on Sundays and hang around together since they were such good friends. Three of the church's were merging because the attendance was too low to keep them open and functioning. On Saturdays each family had obligations and functions that they had to go to. The families would take the kids to the malls until they were old enough to drive themselves. This was a way working class people could relax and enjoy themselves. They had movies theaters, cafes shopping malls, Banks, restaurants and other recreational things going on. This was an outlet for the girls to get out and see some of their friends in the city or the malls and nail salons.

As the girls were growing up and going into junior high school, James and Johnny went on to high school. So, they were at a different school than Brenna and Julie. Brenna and Julie began to see James and Johnny with other girls and this was so upsetting for Brenna because of her crush on James. Again, Brenna had to see and love him from a distance because she was too shy and young to say or remotely tell anyone how she felt. She tried to keep busy and focus all her time on her class work. She became an A student by doing this and had the best grades in her class but kept very much to herself in home room. After a few years had gone by, Brenna and Julie were teenagers watching these young men in high school. They were both fourteen and getting ready to go on to high school as freshmen. James and Johnny were still inundated with lots of young lady's crazy about them. James was always talking to other girls but always made time to come and talk to her. Brenna was so upset with this but she had never even let James know that she was interested in him or how she felt about him. She continued to love him from a distance. Brenna was always day dreaming because she could not let anyone but her friend Julie know that she had such a crush on James. Both Brenna and Julie had met new friends and one young lady, Alice Brantley, the daughter of Robert and Alice Brantley was always talking to them but was never quiet their friend. She seems to want information all the times about James. Alice knew the girls lived near him. Alice told Brenna and Julie that she was interested in James and she knew that James had eyes only for her. Julie spoke up and said that Brenna was also interested in him. When Alice saw that James was paying more attention to Brenna, she would say to her friends that Brenna was ugly and stupid and was failing all her classes. Everyone knew that Brenna was a very beautiful girl and was an honor student just shy. Alice's parents lived in another community but rode the bus with the girls every day. Brenna and Julie knew Alice's parents very well from the church outings and school functions they all attended. They were very nice people to be around but Alice had the most hateful ways and disposition than anyone she had known.

Weekend after weekend Brenna endured Alice and the other girls all over James and this hurt her so much. James noticed that Brenna had stop smiling at him and he started waiting for her every day to get on the school bus and this was how they started talking again. He noticed there was something different about Brenna. She was growing into a beautiful young lady and he really liked her very much. It seemed like this happened overnight. Brenna was very shy in school and James tried talking to her so she would smile more often because she had the most beautiful smile. What a nice young lady with lots of things going for herself. She was very smart, witty and had a level head on her shoulders. She spoke of going to college and getting a degree when she graduates high school. She was very withdrawn but would perk up when she saw him. He liked this about her.

Alice did not like James spending all his time with Brenna. When James was with Brenna, Alice would come up and get into their conversation. This was not working for Alice and she decided to torture Brenna with her snide remarks and malicious lies about her. This went on for a while and then she became interested in someone else or so they thought she did, but she found a way to be nasty to Brenna. Alice broke off her relationship with the other young man and was back stirring up trouble for Brenna and James. Alice Brantley saw that James had become interested in Brenna and she had to stop it before it became too serious as she wanted him for herself. When Brenna saw that Alice was back and starting trouble all over again, Brenna's conversation became limited with James and she stopped talking to him completely. James had not noticed that Alice was causing trouble for Brenna and did not understand why Brenna stopped talking to him. He asked Julie what was going on with Brenna and Julie finally spoke up and told James that Alice was getting into Brenna's face over him. Brenna was now fifteen and James was seventeen and had really dropped all his girlfriends and stopped talking to Alice completely because he only had eyes for Brenna.

Brenna was so excited that James asked her on a date. WOW, he was getting bold as Brenna saw it. He smiled at her and took her hand and kissed her and she thought her heart would explode. Brenna knew he was meant for her. He could not wait to see her because he knew he was in love with her and the minute he saw her and that beautiful smile they were in each other's arms. For Brenna the love from a distance was getting within arm reach for her.

They begin dating off and on for a while but there was always something coming between them. Brenna discovered that James was seeing another girl. She was not sure if it was serious or not. He told Brenna that he was just hanging out and the girl was just there. What James failed to mention that the young lady was Alice? Brenna was just fed up with him and this Alice, and this was grounds for breakup. He tells Brenna it was nothing but Alice decided to let him know that she was back in his life and Brenna needed to know it and accept it. Alice meant to torture Brenna but Brenna began to fight back with kindness. Whenever Alice would say something nasty to Brenna, she would answer her with kindness and this would make her more upset at Brenna. Julie knew that Alice was being promiscuous with a number of young men at school but she did not want to hurt her by saying it to her. Brenna did tell her at one point that young men did not like to marry young ladies that they can have their way with at any time and this was not Christ like and Alice told her to mine her business and continued her behavior with the boys at high school. Slowly Brenna pretended not to care what James did although it was breaking her up inside.

Brenna and James split up for a while and James became very quiet and distant and he let Brenna know that he was not interested in **Alice Brantley** and did not care for her at all and that he only had eyes for her. James had asked Brenna on a date to the movies and she had accepted. Alice confronted Brenna and James at the movie theater and the scene was very ugly. Neither one of them knew how Alice found them at the movies. James would not let Brenna speak or get involved and told Alice that he was not interested in her and she needed to move on. She became belligerent with both of them and told them that they would pay for hurting her and that it was not over between them. James and Brenna rekindled their relationship and kissed and made up. James was very careful with her and did not pressure her into going all the way because he knew she was a Christian girl and the kind of girl he wanted for his wife. They continued dating until James finished high school and was getting ready for college. They saw each other every day until James went off to college where he studied to be an electrical engineer. Alice moved on to Florida and married a young man **Terrance Black** whom she met a few years later at college. None of us knew Terrance Black because he did not live in the area. Alice and Terrance had a baby the first year they were married and James and Brenna kind of lost touch with Alice. This was fine with Brenna because all she gave her was sheer foolishness. Brenna knew that with James moving on to college that he could find another girl and drop her anytime. She loved him so much and almost changed her mind about the college she wanted to go too.

While James was in college, he dated other girls and they both made it abundantly clear that if they decided to move on with other people that it would be ok because at this point, they were very young and needed to date other people before settling down. Neither had a problem with it. Even though James made this decision to date other people he was not happy with the decision at all, but he could not say too much because it was his decision to do this. It was after he came home and saw how beautiful Brenna was, he changed his mind about her dating other people. While he was in school all he could see was his Brenna dating someone else or in someone else arms. This was totally tearing him apart but he had to bear it.

During the summer James and Brenna were inseparable. While James was home Brenna had a boyfriend Williams Lawrence that did not like her dating James when he came home from college and tried to convince her that he would only go back to his college friend. Brenna broke it off with William Lawrence because he was becoming too jealous of her and James. She had explained that she had a boyfriend and he was alright with it but when James came home, he wanted to change the relationship. James did not like him because he thought there was something about him that was not Christian like.

What James and Brenna both discovered about themselves that absence makes the heart grow fonder? Brenna and James kissed every time they got a chance. Brenna could not get enough of kissing James and being in his arms. They planned everything around each other. He knew that Brenna was the only person for him. Even with him dating in college he was only happy with Brenna. He really loved this girl and she loved him. Although they had other friends when he was home, they did not see other people at all. He knew she was a virgin and did not plan to have sexual relations with her until marriage. This was fine with him because he wanted this as well. They could wait until marriage.

They went to church and worked diligently with each other during the summer helping children. They worked on summer vacation packages for the youth at their respected churches and sometime together on other projects. James wanted Brenna to come to college when she graduated, with him but she was not sure about this because he had been there for two years. She wanted her degree to be in Accounting with a concentration in Business Management. She just was not sure this would be a good idea. Especially with him having dated other girls there. Brenna thought that this would be too much of a distraction. Brenna did not worry about James interest in other girls because she gave it to the Lord when he left for college and said that if God meant for them to be together, he would work it out for them. She was in her last year of high school with a month before graduation.

James was not too happy about her picking another college to go to. She is beginning to see that James has a trust issue with her. She reminded him that she only loves him and he should trust her decision as she trusted him and his decision of the college of his choice. James never mention the issue with the college again as he learned to trust her judgment on where she wanted to go. Like she told him he put it in God's hand and concentrated on his degree. The college she wanted to go too had to have a great accounting department. She was looking at the Ivy League colleges because she knew that they had great curriculums in accounting.

Brenna, has been accepted at Goshen College, Statesman's Univ., University of Salter, Dale, Delton Univ., and Vander University and several more. Brenna loved Vander Univ. She later accepted a scholarship to Vander Univ., and James was not too happy but he has accepted the fact that she would be going on to Vander Univ.

James for the last two years has been concentrating on his studies and thinking of the days that he will be together with Brenna. He has been dating often and on but nothing serious. There are two or three girls, Danielle, Loren, and Tamika that has made a play for him but he just is not interested in a love relationship with any one of them. He has gone out with Tamika Carter a few times and she is well aware of Brenna because James has told her all about Brenna. Some weekends he travels home to see Brenna. One of the girls in particular Tamika Carter, has vowed to make him fall for her but he talks to Brenna so often that she stays on his mind and nothing Tamika says sways him. He is head over heels in love with Brenna. Tamika tells her friend that she really likes James but he has no interest in her or anyone other than Brenna. Well she hopes this Brenna does not break his heart because he is a really nice young man.

On Sundays he goes to church on campus and he does the worship and praise there. He just loves the Lord so much that he can't stay away from the Church and Tamika does not like to go to church. This is a turn off for James because he was brought up in church and loves hearing Gods word.

On Thursday evening he has a bible session with some of the students on campus that enjoy Gods word like himself. Sometimes Tamika will show up but just to talk to James. He thinks that if she continues to come to the session, she will eventually begin to have a love for Christ herself. So, for she continues to come to the session. She is a lovely girl and James thinks that she will someday come around to Christ. She asks a lot of questions all the time about Christ and she is more intrigued about how he died for us and rose that we might have a right to live. He has explained how God loves all of us. She says her parents never took an interest of Church and they never went to church as a family. James knew that this could happen and if you are never taught about God you won't know anything about him. James explain to **Tamika** that you keep Him first in your life things will happen that you never even dreamed of. But you must have a love for Christ and learn how to study Gods word. When you study his Word, his Word will get in you. James told Tamika about Jesus being God's son and how he had his only son to die that we might have a right to live. Tamika finally moved on and started dating someone out of the Bible session and she really has changed and enjoys the session like all the kids there. James was so happy that she had found someone that she had an interest in and certainly not him. He did not want his life complicated when it came to Brenna. Tamika had a break through and decided to follow the path of God. What a Blessing for her and Franklin was so pleased with her decision and he remembers that God said to go after the one lost sheep. His answers speak volumes.

James has graduated and started his MBA program and Brenna is now in her third year at Vander University. Now she and James are engaged and looking forward to getting married in a year. James is back in college at Statesman's Univ., and has focused all of his time to his class work and getting all A's. He is now working on his MBA. Brenna is now at Vander Univ.; third year and all her time and energy is focused on her class work. Her work ethics always comes natural to her and it pays off with good grades. James has driven to Nashville to campus to see her on many occasions. They are in the planning stages of their wedding.

Brenna has met another young man at Vander, Franklin McClean and they are keeping it real as he is also engaged to his fiancé' Adrianna Johnson. She missed James so much but loving him from a distance was working for them now. So, Brenna and Franklin both just challenge each other with homework so they don't get involved with other people. Their student friends thought they were an item but it was totally great friendship. They managed to keep this a secret from their friends and it worked out perfectly. So, for this has worked out for Brenna and James. They talk about their friends all the time and the love they have for each other. Our fiancé's James and Adrianna visits us around the same time so we can get to know each other. Adrianna is at the Univ., of Salter and she will be graduating a year ahead of Brenna and Julie. The four of them became great friends and plan to be in each other's weddings. They are all Christians and it's great that they found each other in school. When you are in college you meet all types of people but it was something about Franklin that drew Brenna to him. She always talked about the love of Jesus Christ and this is when she understood that he was a Christian as well. Brenna was astounded when Franklin let her know that he is a young minister and goodness this is just great. He has had Brenna's back on several issues in class and she can definitely count on him. James is very happy that Brenna is protected by a Christian person Franklin at college as well. I think that God put them together for a reason. Arianna, Franklin fiancé" have not met Julie yet but plan to meet when the semester is over. She will be visiting the home of Brenna so they can continue planning the wedding for the four of them.

Brenna never knew that she could love someone so very much but James made it so very easy to love. He has the most beautiful brown eyes and his smile will melt your heart. James and Brenna are not perfect people but they both have a love for Christ Jesus and they know this is what keeps them grounded. They both worked part time with companies in their field of study while they are in college. They both know what they wanted to do once they graduate from college. Both have great work ethics and this should take them very far in life.

Julie and Johnny attended Goshen College and she and Johnny split after her first year. She is still Brenna's best friend but they don't get to see each other until they are home from college in the summer. Julie met a nice young man Kevin Snow whom she is smitten with and they too are talking marriage. He lives in a town near their home now but he is originally from Syracuse, NY. He has family in the area and has always wanted to live in the South. One of his family members invited him to stay with them until he got an apartment, which he did. Kevin also have a love for the church. He was the worship leader in his church back in Syracuse.

The way Julie and Brenna were raised they both looked for young men of Christian faith. Their parents instilled that into them as they were growing up. It does not work all the time but with Brenna she found a love in James and Julie and Johnny did not work. They both found new love with other people. Johnny has graduated and is working for a fortune 500 company and doing very well. He did not continue on with his MBA but plans to go back and get it within two years, but at a different college. Johnny felt that staying at Goshen would present another problem since Julie is still at the college. It was time for him to move on.

Brenna and Julie were thick as thieves planning Brenna's wedding to James and their new friends Franklin McClean and Arianna White.

They are wondering how this is going to work with Johnny being in the wedding as well. Johnny has a new love interest Camille Wheeler. Brenna remain friends with him and his new love interest Camille although she and Julie are best friends. Brenna has met Camille and found her to be a very nice young lady as well. Brenna and James knew that Johnny and Julie had split in college but they just don't know if it was a hostile breakup or mutually done.

On getting to know Camille Wheeler and seeing her interaction with Johnny has come as a relief to Brenna and knowing Julie and her Christian ways she will get along with Camille as well. With the holidays fast approaching and everyone getting ready to travel home, Julie is looking forward to meeting up with all her friends and enjoying the holiday. Even Alice is coming home and has let some of her friends know that she will be in town. No one has heard anything from her since she went off to college and got married to a young man there in Florida her first year of college. Upon Brenna hearing this, she knew she had to have her guard up at all times not offensive but alert. Whenever Alice is on the scene, there is always trouble on the horizon. Brenna knows that Alice will do anything to get James back and this worries her although she knows how James feel. Brenna does not like confrontations and will walk away from any situation rather than stand up for herself. Julie is always telling her that she needs to stand up and don't be a push over for anyone. Brenna knows full well that God can fix anything if it's meant to be. Brenna have come to the realization in her life now that she is engaged to James and she has to be more aggressive where James is concerned and let Alice know that James is her fiancé and they are going to be married in a short period of time regardless of any interference from her. Alice needs to get over it and move on. James is off limits to her now and there is no three people in a marriage. Brenna is wearing the ring and it will be Brenna and James only. Brenna is coming into her own where James is concern and not the typical quiet little girl as she was back in high school. She is totally responsible for her life, her man, and keeping him. She has to learn not to be a stepping stone for anyone. Brenna knows this but sometimes she gets a little timid where Alice is concerned and goes back into her shell.

Julie knows that if she continues to speak up and not be so timid, she can conquer anything. Alice knows just how to push Brenna's buttons to the point that Brenna just shuts down. She knows Alice plan to come home this year for Thanksgiving because her mom saw Brenna's mom and told her that she would be coming home. So, Brenna is really dreading the meeting between her and Alice. She just doesn't know what to expect from Alice when she sees her. It has been communicated around Atlanta that Brenna and her friends are coming home and planning the event for the thanksgiving holidays. Her mother has told them that Alice would be home with her husband and baby.

CHAPTER
TWO

The Holidays

James and Johnny's grandparents are preparing for the arrival of their grandchildren and has starting baking for the Thanksgiving holiday dinner. They are so excited that James and Brenna are engaged and cannot contain themselves. They too can't wait to start planning for their wedding.

Johnny will be home later in the day as he is spending his day with his new girlfriend Camille Wheeler. Johnny's friend is from their home and only live a short distance away in another community, thou they never met until they went off to college. They will be home for dessert on Thanksgiving Day. Everyone is rushing around getting ready for the program but their parents are not aware of the program that has been planned that evening by their children. They will be truly blessed by Julie's fiancé Kevin Snow. Franklin McClean and Arianna also live in the area and everyone will be here for the worship service. Franklin will be bringing the message and this is the first time any of the group has had the pleasure of hearing and seeing him stand in front of a congregation of people to preach.

James and Brenna arrive home because their classes ended earlier and they could leave campus. James drove to pick up Brenna on the way to their home. He spent about an hour there at Vander Univ., with Brenna and her friends Franklin McClean and his friend Arianna. The two of them Franklin and Arianna were leaving later on that evening. As Brenna and James left campus, they were now on the road home. They arrived home and James immediately left for his grandparents' home so he could relax and take a nap from the drive. Brenna was very tired and relaxed with her parents and her siblings for a few hours catching them up on college life on the campus of Vander University.

Now that they both have had a few hours of rest and relaxation they head out to the church to put together their plans for Thanksgiving Eve service. This year the service is at Brenna's church and her Pastor has allowed her to be master of ceremony for Thanksgiving Eve service. She has a special guest Lined up to perform at their service. She is so excited and can't wait to tell James, Johnny and Julie who has agreed to sing at the service for them. Kevin Snow, Julie's fiancé is a worship leader in his church in Syracuse, NY. Since he is coming home with Julie for Thanksgiving, to meet her family, Brenna has talked him into singing with them at her church on Thanksgiving Eve. Julie knows that Kevin will bring the house down with his great voice. Kevin will be recording his first CD during the Christmas Holidays. The Eight of them, Brenna, James, Kevin, Julie, Arianna, Johnny, Camille and Franklin will be opening up the service for their pastor and they are so excited about doing this for their parents. Franklin has agreed to preach for Brenna's Pastor, Rev. Dereck Hoffman. Pastor Hoffman is so gracious in allowing this young man to bring the Sermon for Thanksgiving service. Brenna had recorded one of Minister Franklin McClean sermon and sent it to Pastor Dereck Hoffman and he liked the young man so well he called him and asked him to do the sermon for the Service. The eight of them have not rehearsed together but they all have the same CD and has been practicing with it. Camille has come aboard and can really sing too. She has become an integral part of their group of friends since she's been dating Johnny. Johnny and James have agreed to accompany the group as they sing. They are all very talented musicians and singers in their own right. They all play an instrument but don't have the time to use their musical skills very much since they have been in college but they can make some beautiful music together. When they are home during the summer months, Franklin, Brenna,

Julie, and Kevin performs together on weekends to help fund part of their project for their future studio. However, they're hoping that these performances that they are doing will let them know whether they can become a professional group of singers after college.

Brenna called James and they made their way over to her Pastor's home to finalize their plans for Thanksgiving eve service. They met with Brenna's Pastor and he has welcomed all of their fresh ideas. He thought they were amazing for the service. All he could say was well something new for this year and he loved it. Kevin is a young minister and loves sharing his love for Christ with everyone. Their plans are to be a great blessing to the church for Thanksgiving Holiday.

James calls out to Brenna to go out with him for lunch at Swazi's Grille and catch a movie later that evening as he just needed some alone time with Brenna to kiss her and tell her how much he loves her and can't wait to be married to her. He knows that Alice will be in town and trouble will start with her and he does not want to get into any unpleasantness with her and Brenna. This time he will have to set her straight because Brenna is it for him and he will never let anyone else come between them now. They are a solid couple ready to be married and settled. James would not let Alice or anyone hurt Brenna ever again.

Finally, it is Thanksgiving eve and the eight of them are rushing around in the choir room before the worship and praise begins. Brenna comes out with Julie and introduces everyone to the congregation. Brenna starts the song and Julie, Kevin, James and Johnny chimes in. They get through the worship and praise part of the service and the program is in full swing. It is now time for the entire group to perform. Kevin Snow comes out and sings first and what a blessing it was for him to perform. The eight of them perform together and the entire church is on their feet clapping and singing along with them. Now it is time for Pastor Hoffman to introduce Minister Franklin McClean as minister for the Thanksgiving service. After the introduction, Kevin gave the most beautiful rendition of a song for the holiday. Then Minister Franklin is up, first he prays and he is giving the scripture and then the title of his sermon which is **SHARING WITH OTHERS.** One of the most beautiful messages that Brenna had heard him preach. It was so appropriate for the Thanksgiving holiday. The entire evening was simply great. Even Alice was in the audience of her church for the program and commented on the program. All of the other churches came together at Brenna's church and the entire evening was awesome. Everyone loved the program that had been put together by Brenna and her friends. Everyone was so excited about how the program went and wanted to talk to all of them about how beautiful they all sang and how long had they been performing together as a group.

Julie's and Brenna's parents were so happy after the concert that they couldn't stop talking about it. They thought all of the kids that performed were excellent. Brenna's mom couldn't stop saying I told you that you could do this if you only trust him and look you did. You girls were brilliant up there. God is so pleased with the work that you all continue to do in his name. What a Blessing to this community.

Alice seemed a little frustrated and not happy at all but Brenna thought that with being married and still in school with a baby could be the issue but she kind of gave Brenna the impression that there was trouble in Paradise. Brenna did not entertain that conversation because she thinks Alice is up to her old tricks again. Alice seem to be very friendly and was impressed with the program that had been presented at the church. She introduced everyone to her husband Terrance and their son Terrence Jr. Her immediate family was in the audience as well. She asked Brenna if she could speak to her and Brenna knew at this time it was something negative that she had to say. Well she spoke briefly to Brenna of having marital problems at the time and she still had eyes for James. Brenna knew that this time she had to say something back to Alice. Brenna let Alice finish telling her not to get too comfortable with her up-coming nuptials because she is still close around. Brenna told Alice that she thought she had a very nice husband, very handsome and very attentive to her and her child and that she should be thankful to God that she had such and be appreciative of what she has oppose to staying in other people lives and business and trying to get a rise out of them. Alice was shocked that Brenna spoke up. Brenna is not worried now because her self-esteem has been rejuvenated and life is great right now between James and herself. What a shame that Alice has such a nice young husband, but to try and ruin it for Brenna as well. Alice will always be the most selfish person and if she doesn't change her attitude, she will lose a nice husband being selfish. Brenna was not letting her get to her on this night because they had just come down off a high in church. There is an old saying is to keep your friends close and your enemies closer. She was very kind to Alice and told her that she would be praying for her. What Brenna didn't know was that Alice was very envious of Brenna and the rest of the group. She wanted to be performing with the group as well but she never spoke up and told anyone. She thought that maybe one of them would ask her if she could sing and she really can sing.

Terrence, Alice's husband is a young man well-spoken and grew up in the Washington, DC area. He told all of them that he and Alice planned to move back to Atlanta, GA in January. as his job is transferring him there and that Alice would be living with one of her cousins or his parents in Florida to finish up this semester. She could not get all of her classes that she had signed up for on line so she did not really have an option but to stay to finish up. Alice would be spending the next four and a half (4 1/2) to five months in Florida. She and Terrence have the only grandchild and they want him to be close to his grandparents. She has applied to some of the colleges there in Atlanta so maybe she will be doing her last semester in Atlanta with her husband and son. She is going to summer school in Atlanta, GA to be able to transfer on into her last year without any problems. Alice may want to stay in Florida to finish up. One thing Brenna can say is that they were all good students in high school and did very well to get into some of the best colleges.

They were all invited back to Julie's house for coffee and dessert after the concert. Brenna even invited Alice and her husband to join them as well. She refused to go to Brenna's at first but her mom and dad told her to go on and enjoy her friends that they would take care of their grandchild. Alice and her husband Terrence agreed to go for coffee and dessert with them. Brenna informed Alice that they planned on going to the Jazz Club after dessert and she and Terrence is also invited there with them. The group went on to the jazz club to listen to music, dance and then to perform if asked too. Sometime the club would have open MIC and they would take the opportunity to sing with each other. Alice and Terrence came with them and she totally surprised them all. While they were having open MIC, Alice got up and sang a song and she was really good, something none of them expected. She sang so well that the Ensemble asked her to sing with them the next few songs if she knew them. She did so and she really liked performing with them. A light bulb went off and Brenna knew why Alice did not care for her and found every opportunity to go after her because she wanted to be a part of the group and they did not let her in. Maybe If they let her in all the turmoil with her will be over. If there ever was an 'Aha-moment it was the minute Alice opened her mouth and started to sing. It was great and another way of adding to the group and maybe even having a solo artist. Alice never knew how to tell them she could sing as well and would love to be a part of the ENSEMBLE. Brenna's mom always told her that God will work everything out just keep on trusting in him and keep him first in your life. Look what God did?

With Alice moving back to Atlanta this will work out perfectly for the Ensemble and as soon as she gets settled, she needs to come aboard and start rehearsing with them to get acclimated into the group. Her mom and dad would be an integral part in their grandson's life as she travels with the ENSEMBLE. Terrence is good in sales and maybe later on he would be a person to manage and work on sales for their CD's in their recording studio, or he can continue on with his business career with the company that he is with. This is a year and a few months away before Julie and Brenna can know what is going on with the studio.

The group wants Alice to start recording with them in Syracuse during spring Break. But they are going to leave it up to Alice because she has a lot to do with the move from Florida and deciding whether to stay in school in Florida or move to Atlanta and look for a college. She maybe too late to get into a college here in Atlanta. All of this will totally be left up to Alice. The group hopes that she has the same week of spring break as they have and this will work out perfectly. What they have discovered about Alice is that she has all this talent and never used it at all. She really has a beautiful voice just waiting to be tested and recorded. However, what the ENSEMBLE is doing for Alice, they are sending her the Christmas CD to learn all the songs for the Christmas concert.

As they are all packing and getting ready to travel back to college for their finals Brenna is well into her plans for their Christmas concert which they are planning with all the choirs in the area to come together and give one big concert for the surrounding communities and then travel back home for the Christmas Holidays and present the concert.

All flyers have been printed and distributed in all the communities and all have been asked to donate Clothing, can goods, goods in boxes, and even money donations so that goods could be bought to be distributed to the homeless on Saturday before Christmas Eve. Some other churches heard what was been done in the area for the homeless and wanted to help in any way they could. They donated food and clothing as well. Some company donated two hundred (200) coats to be given out to the needy families. There is no fee to get into the concert, however everyone needs to bring can goods as a donation.

Brenna, James, Julie and Johnny are coordinating the concert with the church organist to pull this concert off. All are very cooperative in doing their share in the organizing and putting all the songs together. Each director for the churches that's participating are rehearsing their choirs together twice a week so everyone is on the same page on concert night. To their surprise, they even had other churches join in with them along with their organist and the community organist can't wait to tell the group about it. They have over one hundred forty-five (145) people participating in the choir for the concert. This had never been done before and when they all come together and they sound like angels singing together. The group, Brenna, James, Johnny, Camille, Julie, Kevin, Franklin and Arianna have a week a half to rehearse with the choirs.

They will all be together for the Christmas Holidays but Julie and Kevin will be leaving two days after Christmas to be home in Syracuse, NY for the New Year's with his parents and family. Julie is very excited about meeting Kevin's family for the first time. She knows that his father is a Minister and his mom is an Evangelist. Julie's family has talked to Kevin's parents and they are excited as well to meet their son's fiancé Julie. They too are hoping that the two of them will settle in Syracuse. Kevin and Julie have none of those plans. Their plans are to live in Atlanta.

All their Christmas songs are coming together really nicely. Brenna is not worried about the church choirs because their Organist are quite familiar with all the songs, they picked out together and they are well under control. Time is really flying because Brenna has only two (2) more exams which she is taking this morning and she and James will be ready to travel this evening. The College that James attend is not too far from hers, about an hour's drive and then they will be traveling home together for Christmas. Alice has agreed to participate in the concert and to travel with them to Syracuse, NY for the recording. Terrence is traveling with them as well and he's looking forward to the trip as well.

Their decision has been made about the attire the choir will be wearing to perform in, which is a black dress or suit with red corsages with white baby breathe fashion around the corsages. Brenna ordered two hundred (200) corsages over the Thanksgiving holiday break. She and her college friends make these corsages for the gospel choir at college and made money selling them to pay some of their expenses off. The eight of them chipped in and bought the flowers and they were done and sent to her home. They were their waiting on them when they arrived home. Brenna and James are traveling back home on the 14th of December. The rest of their friends will be traveling on the 14th of December all different times. Now everyone has made it back home safely, James and Brenna get some alone time before the rehearsal starts. Johnny wants them to meet at 4:00 PM so they can get into their rehearsal and get out so he can spend some quality time alone with Camille. All their lives are so busy that they don't really get a chance to spend any time with their fiancé's. Johnny, James, Brenna, Julie, Kevin, Arianna, Camille, Alice and Franklin are at the church practicing their songs for the Holiday Concert. The concert is on Sunday December 20th, at 4:00 PM. The Theme for the concert is **The Greatest Gift of All.** The First song was led by Julie Glass. Holy,

Holy, Holy. The entire song was beautiful and appropriate and Julie did a superb job of singing it. The combined choirs along with the group sang the next song and what a great job they did. The group ensemble joined in with them near the end of the song. They did not want to take control of the entire concert they only wanted to sing with them and show them that this could be done every year instead of having thirty (30) to forty (40) people in every church during the holidays trying to put on a concert with limited people. The choir sang the next three songs without our help. Then the Pastor asked if the ensemble would give them at least two or three songs for the church congregation and of course they were happy to do so. Brenna stepped out and started singing the next song and Kevin Snow joined her and they brought the service to another level. Brenna sang so well and was so uplifted that she could not contain herself. James never saw her on such a spiritual high. She kind of surprised everyone and James came over to her side while she was in such a state of praise and worship. The entire church was on their feet clapping and moving and the Liturgical dancers were all over the church dancing and praising God. The entire service was recorded and they are checking it out to see if they can get a CD of the entire service. The church is equipped to do recordings and they have screens that it can be seen as well.

The concert finally ended and they all gathered in the banquet hall of the church. The group, Brenna, James, Julie, Johnny, Alice, Camille, Kevin, Franklin and Arianna knew that they were going to form this gospel group as soon as everyone has completed their degree or even before. Everyone looked at each other and they all knew what was on each other's mind. This was a must. It has just been proven that they can do this as a group. Alice just fell right in as if she was always a part of the group. Brenna's mind was spinning as she was thinking of somethings. She was not ready to tell the group just yet her thoughts. Now Brenna's mind is still working overtime. She is constantly thinking of a name for the group and she can't get it out of her head. She is writing down all of the names that's coming to her right now and if she doesn't hurry up and get it down on paper she is afraid she will forget all that is crowding her brains. The two names that stayed with Brenna is INTOUCH and JOYFUL-JOYFUL. She had written down about twelve (12) but these two stayed on her mind.

Their parents were overjoyed with what they saw presented by their children. They never quiet knew the magnitude of their kid's talent or rather they knew it but hadn't never seen it presented in concert or in church. How can it all be explained to all of them how proud they were? They just could not stop talking about it.

Now back at home, they were on such a spiritual high from the concert that they were almost forgetting that they had to go shopping. The group was planning on all going Christmas shopping at the Mall for Christmas Gifts for their parents, siblings and their finance'. Brenna did her shopping for James and her older siblings, Sister Leah, Kim and Brother Ivan before she left college so she would not have to do everything when she got home. Brenna only had to shop for her parents, George and Ella. All of them agreed to meet up at the town restaurant after they had completed their shopping for their families. Everyone came back around the time they planned on meeting. It is so cool because most of them will be home for Christmas and New Year's. Kevin and Julie left the day after Christmas. After New Year's they all are traveling to Syracuse, NY to meet up with Kevin & Julie for a few days before they have to go back to college.

Kevin is going into the Studio to record and has asked all of the group to come and help him out on a project. They never guessed it would be singing on his recordings in Syracuse. Kevin had told his parents so much about the group and how much talent they have. Kevin's Father Rev. Snow had flown them in to do a concert at his church. They all arrived today and the concert is tomorrow. Brenna is so excited about the trip to New York because she had never been to Syracuse, NY. They also have never done a concert of this magnitude and especially this far away from home. They are beyond excited.

They met at Kevin's parents' home and they are kind of tired from the trip but excited to meet Kevin's parents and be in Syracuse. Actually, Kevin's parents wanted to hear the entire gospel group perform and has told them that their plans are to have their church sponsor them when they are out of college. This is really exciting news for them. They did not know any of this but Kevin had been constantly calling his dad and mom and letting them know what a fantastic group that he has met and performed with. He told his parents that he had met a young lady in college from the same area as the singers and he was madly in love with her and had asked her hand in marriage. Her name is Julie Glass. His parents knew that Kevin was engaged to a girl name Julie but didn't realize that she was one of the singers in the group as well and since he had been in NY for a few days he did not inform them of this because he wanted it to be a complete surprise when the rest of the group arrived on the scene and his parents would get to hear Julie sing with her melodious voice.. Kevin knows that the two (2) girls Brenna and Julie can really sing professionally right now. They all needed time with their finances' right now.

Brenna's mind is working overtime. She is thinking of a name for the group and has a few written down that she needs everyone to look at. Brenna asked each of them to come up with some names as well and they would put them all together and keep pulling them out until one of them has a good feeling or ring to it. The entire group plans to spend at least seven (7) to eight (8) days in Syracuse. They need to call themselves something other than the Group or the Ensemble.

Brenna is tired from the trip and just wants to be alone with James. She came up to him and tells him to come and go for a walk around the community. She was barely out of their friend's sight before she stopped and gave James a hug and kiss. She had waited as long as she could before she needed that kiss from him. She was aching for his lips on hers. She really loved James so much and can't wait to be married to him. Julie also wants to get away with Kevin for a while and they stroll out toward a restaurant to sit snuggle and kiss as well. It's hard being busy all the time and not getting a chance have some alone time with your fiancé. Terrence and Alice are already married and they just like to hang out with each other. They all met a block from Rev. Snow's home and church at the Grille and had a sandwich and coffee. Franklin was going on about New York and how he had never been to Syracuse, NY but had been to NY, City. He and Arianna are so happy and their wedding is two weeks before Brenna's and James. They walked and discussed how they are going to get married at home in Atlanta and he is going to sing for her and Franklin looks at Arianna and gives her a very long kiss. Johnny and Camille just walked, kissed and held hands while every once in a while glancing at each other and stealing a kiss here and there. The group never get to spend much time together but while in Syracuse they plan to take full advantage of this while they are not in the studio rehearsing. Well it turned out that there was absolutely no time for socializing because they had very long hours in the recording studio,

Rev. Snow gets to hear the entire group and is totally amazed how great they are. With them coming out of the south and already so talented that they can go into any studio right now and produce an excellent recording. What surprised Rev. Snow was the voice that came out of Julie's mouth, his future daughter-in-law. When you put Brenna and Julie together, they are magnificent together. Their voices are so powerful. All he could say was my God my God these children got something special here.

The Concert was so beautiful and very well executed. Kevin knew his church and only gave little directions and everyone was on point. What the group has discovered about Brenna is that she is the take charge person. She handled everything with little effort and things came together

Since singing is something that Brenna always wanted to do, she is prepared to work out something for the group. She and Julie have been saving all their money from doing performances near their college for the last three years. Only Julie, James, and Johnny are aware that they are doing this. There plans are to be able to open their own recording studio one day. She has saved up a fair amount of her paycheck without having to dip into the reserves she has started for her business with and so has her friend Julie. They want to be business partners. She never spent a dime of the money because she wanted to work her plan staying on course within a few years of her graduation. She will open up her Recording Studio along with Julie as soon as they are out of college. Neither one of them are aware of their fathers plans in renovating for them their own Studio. Both Brenna and Julie plan to get married within the next four months of her graduating college to James and Julie in the next six months to Kevin. Both girls' weddings have been planned and paid for by their parents. The families planned their kids' college fund and their daughter's funds for their weddings. They were middle class families living rurally in North Atlanta and they knew that the girls could really sing and one day would be recording artist. So, they spared no expense for them as they were growing up.

Their fathers have gotten together and acquired a piece of property with a building that could be renovated for them to build their studio on, in the northern section of Atlanta, about ten (10) miles out. They thought this was a great investment for their children and their families can work within the business itself. This will be cost efficient while they are ironing out and implementing the plans for the business. Their dads are putting together a team of people to get the business started. The girls only have another year and they will be graduating from college.

However, in the meantime, their fathers will see what the deal is with Kevin's father. George Smaller said to Daniel Glass although New York is a perfect place to do recordings and getting it out to the public but being near and around the Atlanta area is equally as great for them. The cost of living is much cheaper in the Atlanta area and building their own studio is fantastic for them and they would not be obligated to anyone with their own studio and renting it out to others when they are not using it or traveling out of state with the group. This too should bring in Revenue for their business. George Smaller, and Daniel Glass were keeping this a secret from the kids. They want this to be a graduation surprise for both girls since they want to be in the business. Brenna's family is great in putting the logistics together with their plan. They can run the entire studio when they include Julie's family.

They're all college educated with a business background. When it all comes together, the group will be happy because, Kevin being engaged to Julie will be able to record in the area as well without being in Syracuse and when they are in the Syracuse, NY area they can record there. They are both musicians in their own right. Throughout their families they have a drummer, keyboardist, Sax player, bass guitarist and lead guitarist, also pianist and flute player. Each of them has a great amount saved up for their venture just hope it's enough to carry their own backing in case they cannot always be in the NY area. However, if they need further backing maybe Rev. Snow can help them out with it. Their parents have a plan to back the kids but none of them are aware of their plan yet and they have a year to put it into play as well as get the Studio renovated and operational. The work on the studio has begun already.

What Brenna and Julie had noticed that their parents had been spending an awful lot of time on the phone with Kevin's parents, Franklin's parents and also talking to each of the singer's parents in the group? Initially they are trying to get cooperation and understanding from all the parents if they are willing to be on board when they build the studio and the other parent's chip in to help sponsor their children when they start recording and traveling. Some of the parents are not financially able to do this because they just don't have the funds. It's ok because the studio will be owned by Brenna and Julie. If they can at least be willing to travel with the group until everyone is financially able to hold their own this would help the group. If not when they all get on their feet, they can help one another. This will work because all of them are great friends now, but don't know what will happen in the future. Brenna knows that somethings never work out according to plans you set in life. Only time will tell or reveal what happens to their ideas, plans and the business.

The guys never talk about what their plans are in singing and playing a role in the business. They too have plans to purchase a bus for the business and as soon as they have a group name that they have agreed on, they will have the bus delivered with all the details on it. They can't wait to see the girl's faces. Johnny's company that he works for makes these buses and he is getting a great discount to buy one of the buses for the groups touring. Everything is set up for them and all the guys are putting a big down payment on the bus and with Johnny's discount they can purchase a brand-new bus for travel. They are just so blessed but they know they owe it all to God. Through his Grace and his mercy, He has allowed good things to happen for them. If the studio is up and running, they can make money by renting out time to other artist for their recordings as well.

None of them has agreed upon the name yet and they are still calling themselves "THE ENSEMBLE". The Ensemble knows that whatever group they form, Brenna will be their manager and if it gets too much for her to manage, she has already suggested her siblings as take-charge individuals and it should work out perfectly for them. The one thing that the Smaller, children were taught earlier in life was about business. Brenna's Sister Kim was the brains and could handle any situation like Brenna. Leah too was the financial side and Ivan is the computer Genius. So, they are all business minded kids. Johnny has two sisters that could also come aboard with the Ensemble and help out as well as Julie's sister Dawn, and a brother Brian. The entire group has family that can come and help them run any business they set up.

However, they are in New York and working everyday with Kevin on his CD. They work six (6) to ten (10) hours a day and it has been just exhausting. None of them have very much experience when it comes to recording. Only Kevin has that experience but with them working with him they are getting their fair share of what it takes to be a recording artist. Thank God for the Studio being owned by Kevin's father, they have all the time they needed or wanted to record. Rev. Snow saw this in his son early on and decided to build a studio for him just to record for himself and the church. What Rev. Snow also saw in this group of singers was natural talent, something that every one of them possess. This was the most amazing news that they have ever experienced. Brenna could not wait to call her parents and inform them of their good news. It seems like the closer they get to graduating college, positive things are beginning to happen for the group. Brenna said it best that God is an Amazing and Awesome God, and if you let him use you and be obedient to his word, he will give you the desires of your heart. Just trust him and see what happens in your life.

CHAPTER
THREE

Their trip to Syracuse was wonderful and exciting at the same time, but they are back in Atlanta and packing for their trip back to college for the winter and spring semester. As James is pulling up to her dorm, she can see that he is very tired. He is completely exhausted. Brenna is immediately concerned about him and called her friend Franklin to take James into his dorm for the evening so he can get some much-needed rest before traveling the hour (1) to his dorm. He still has a day left before he has to be back in his dorm. Franklin agreed to let James stay in his apartment with him. Brenna was so thankful to Franklin for helping her out. They cannot have overnight quest in the girl's dorms and Brenna did not need the trouble because the RA's would certainly report her. Franklin has become good friends with James and don't mind helping Brenna out. They had worked very hard in Syracuse and didn't get any rest at all and they are still running around but have no time to rest before class starts. They certainly won't be taking on any engagements for a couple of weeks because they need rest right now. Franklin and Arianna flew in from Syracuse and they did not have to go back home for clothes. They packed his car before they left and his brother drove it back for them as he lives in Nashville himself. Brenna will certainly fly out from Nashville during the spring break so she won't be so exhausted after the recording as well. James called Brenna very early the next morning to let her know that he was leaving and not to get out of bed because she needed her rest as well and that he loved her very much and would see her at Spring break. They're both back at their dorms getting ready to delve into their last semester of college third year.

Kevin and Julie were so happy with the progress he's made on the CD. She called Brenna with the news of Kevin's project. They are both screaming, crying and shouting of their excitement for Kevin. Julie tells Brenna that they have to travel back to Syracuse again to finalize the recording for Kevin's CD. They only have to do a small amount of work and it will be done, although Brenna have to do the duet with Kevin and Julie is doing a solo on the CD for her finance'. Brenna finished her solo when she was in Syracuse. Kevin's dad is sending those round trips tickets for the group during spring break. They have asked Alice to do her song that she wrote which is beautiful so that can be added on the CD too. She was way out in left field but God had a way of bringing her in and using her as well. Rev. Snow wants all the tracks done with all song completely finished. They know the CD will be good because they heard all the tracks without all components and it sounds great and beautiful. So with all components added in, along with all artists it will be a great CD. They are all gearing up and getting excited again about the trip back to Syracuse to record.

Kevin has asked Brenna to come up with a name for his new CD. She took one look at all the songs and said **IN TOUCH WITH HIM** and then **HIGHER IN JESUS and Experiencing God's love.** Kevin said I like it, Higher in Jesus. This is letting me know that I am taking my relationship with Jesus Christ Higher. For me this is perfect, it is saying it all for me. Brenna likes it but she tells Kevin to keep an open mind and let her think about it again. Another one is **God's Love is real.** She is not set with that name Higher in Jesus yet but God's Love is Real register more in her spirit. It has somehow resonated in her spirit, mine and soul. Brenna asked the group for their input and so for they are thinking of names. We probably will stay with the name Higher in Jesus since Kevin likes it so much. Brenna will pray on this for a while and see what the Lord will show her. But she loves the Lyrics in Experiencing God's Love.

Brenna and all her friends are well into their last semester of their third year and they're packing again for spring break. None of them are going home for their spring break, they are headed to Syracuse, NY for the final touches of Kevin's CD. It will be coming out in the summer if they're successful with all the recordings during the break. The Ensemble have a week to pull it together. Their plane landed in Syracuse early morning and they will rest for two (2) hours and then off to the studio. Alice is recording with them in NY and has agreed to sing the song she has written. She sang the song perfect the very first time and then they started putting all the parts to it. She ended up going back to the hook because Kevin wanted to record that section again. The timing was slightly off after all voices were added on. What the entire group learned, that singing and recording is definitely not an easy task. It is very hard work. Brenna and Julie went over their song. All the girls have naturally beautiful voices and either one of the girls can take a song and perform it beautifully. The group that they have is spirit filled and can sing anything. Their first day went very well and tomorrow they will work on other sections of the CD as background singers for Kevin. He is just an amazing singer and can play the keyboard as well as he can sing with little effort. He is so talented and they don't know what they are going to do when he start all his recordings and traveling as well. It's going to be very hard to replace him because their group knew he was going to have a Solo career. Day two starts with them putting finishing touches on their recordings. Everything went well on the second and third day. Day four brought out everyone's nerves and tempers was flying left and right, so Kevin thought it was a good idea for them to call it a day and start fresh the next day. On the last day everybody was upbeat and apologizing for the day before and the finishing touches was completely done within a couple of hours and they relaxed and listen to the CD and the Studio personnel thought it was a rap and was a very good CD. They would know soon enough once the CD comes out into the stores. It was time for them to travel back home the next day and they all just wanted to hang out with their fiancés. Brenna and James chose to go to a little restaurant down town Syracuse for a date night and some alone time. Each one of the couples had their own plans for the evening. James and Brenna couldn't wait to be alone just to be in each other's arms again. They loved each other so much and lately it seems like all they ever do is sing record and work. This trip was very important to all of them and they had to finish it up for Kevin because they promised him, they would help him do the project. Brenna wanted a steak dinner and James decided on lobster. Dinner was very good and they really enjoyed themselves. James and Brenna had not been out together since the holidays and this was great for them to be out together. Franklin, Arianna, Johnny, Camille, Alice and her husband Terrence all went out to a restaurant in another section of Syracuse that Kevin told them about. All of them had spent their entire spring break working and not resting and when they get back to college it began all over again for them, college classwork and really get back into their schedule because they only have two months to prepare for their last semester Exams. Julie and Kevin had dinner with his family and then they just had a very long talk with his parents about their wedding and where they wanted to live after they finished college. His parents wanted them to come back to Syracuse and live there because he had invested so much into the studio. Kevin is not happy with his father's plans on him living in Syracuse. He wants to continue living in the Atlanta area. It is less expensive to live in Atlanta than in Syracuse. The housing is much cheaper and you get much more property for the homes in Atlanta, plus he likes Atlanta very much. Kevin wants to build a second studio in Atlanta and he plans to tell his parents of his plans when he graduates college. He can work in the studio when he is home with his parents and he can hire some of the people from the church to continue running the studio there in Syracuse. He can send work to the studio there and continue running his studio in Atlanta. Kevin is thinking ahead that he can run the business from New York and run the one also in Atlanta. Kevin knows that Atlanta is a great area to have a studio and it will bring in lots of revenue. What Kevin doesn't know is that Brenna and Julie's parents are already working on the recording studio for the two girls. Each of them has expressed an interest of having their own recording studio, but does not know that their parents are well into renovating the place that they purchased for them to turn it into a studio.

The entire group has returned to Kevin's parents' home to sit and reflect on the CD that Kevin has just completed. They're all in a very good mood and the vibe among them are really great. They are leaving tomorrow evening to head back to Nashville and some of them are headed back to Atlanta. James and Brenna are packed already and just a few items are left out for them to change into for their trip back to college. Overall, it was a great time in Syracuse for them but Brenna is still wound up about the Soloist part. James tried to calm her down with telling her that she will have time to think about it when she gets settled back at her dorm. She wished James was near her dorm instead of an hour away. She just needs him by her side. He laughs and tells Brenna, I told you to come to the same college with me and she only smiles and wishes she had but then she would not have met Franklin and Arianna.

They are on the plane in the air now back to Nashville for them and Brenna can't wait until she is back in her dorm and in her bed for the evening. She is very tired from the trip and all the recordings. She has two more months and she can take some time off to rest for a week or two. They still have to wait to hear from Kevin about them touring this summer with him. It would be nice if they already knew what their plans was with this but unfortunately, they have to wait. James drove himself back to his dorm and he was tired as well and needed rest. Spring break is over and they officially have to be back in their classrooms on Monday. Julie and Kevin flew out with James and Brenna because they all are flying into Nashville to go to their respective college dorms. Julie notice that Kevin seems a bit upset about something and waited until they were flying to ask what it was all about and he explained that he wants to live in Atlanta but his parents wants him to come home and run the studio there in Syracuse. He tells Julie that he only agrees to do this for a couple of months and after they get married, he plans to move indefinitely back to Atlanta. Julie doesn't mine either way but it certainly will affect her opening up her studio at home with Brenna. Julie is upset now and he is holding her and kissing her and telling her it's going to be ok. She loves Kevin very much. It's a lot that has to be discussed between them once they get out of college and settled. So, Kevin tells Julie not to worry about it now that they have a whole year to decide what they are going to do. She explains her plans to Kevin about going into business with Brenna when they graduate. This was always a plan that she and Brenna wanted. Kevin is kind of shocked because he thought that she would be willing to go into business with him but that hadn't been discussed either. There's a lot that needs to be worked out before the wedding and they get settled in whatever area they are going to live in. On the way from the airport to the dorm Kevin is thinking that maybe the four of them could go into business together. He will discuss this with Julie and Brenna after he deals with his upcoming CD. He knows that his manager Father and Mother will handle all of the business with the CD that's coming out. Kevin wants to talk to the Ensemble about being his background singers. He knows that they want to form their own group and be on their own but until they get this settled, he's hoping that they will work with him. With them backing him on his CD it will be wonderful and he won't have to take on all new artists to work with. They all have a chemistry together and it works. They are all back in their respective dorms from Spring Break. Brenna will call everyone on Monday evening to let them know they need to meet real soon.

Kevin has finished his first CD and they know it's just a matter of time before Kevin starts out on his tour for his CD. The group is not sure yet if they will be touring with him. The opportunity has not presented itself to the group yet whether they will be on tour with him. Well it seems like either Franklin, James or Johnny will have to step up and learn how to be soloists and worship leaders at the same time. The guys all have natural good voices and can be trained to really become good lead singers. They had expressed their concerns about this but Brenna mind is working overtime again. Her suggestion is to start the guys now with their training or get Kevin to train them to be soloists. They can bring in a trainer to help or maybe Kevin knows someone that can step in and help the group with this. Brenna also knows that her brother Ivan can also train in that area as well. He is the worship and praise leader in their own church, however will he have the time to do it. Ivan can sing as well but he likes the logistics part of the business-like computers and other areas of the recording business. When there were problems and they needed another singer, he would step in and perform and the group would never miss a beat. Maybe Ivan will have to learn how to be one of the soloists for the group as well. He already knows many of their songs so it was never a problem for him to perform. Our parents taught us how to harmonize and be a group among ourselves. Even her sisters were trained to sing as well and there were never any worries about being without a singer. So, if there was anything going on with the group, they would call on Brenna to solve their problem. This was Brenna being Brenna taking control. Brenna called a meeting and brought this subject up and the group looked at her and said what is wrong with you, this is something you are very good at. Brenna never saw herself in this role because she was too busy trying to see who could do it other than herself. James reminded her that she could handle it and her sisters could join in and be a great asset to the group as well. The funniest thing about all the families that grew up together, they all have a singing background and all can really sing. Franklin did not grow up with them but Brenna had met him in college and found out that he lived in the general area just not in their community. He is a great guy and minister. He can be a great worship leader as well as soloist for the group. With Franklin they just have to remember that he is a minister first and if he is called to a church, they have to be able to continue to grow and move on if this happens. This would have to be something Franklin have to deal with when he graduates this May. Franklin has been going to summer school every year for Seminary and this is very important to him. Brenna knows that Franklin has been preparing for this for a while and they have to respect his wishes of being a minister.

The entire group has thoughts going through their heads about what they are going to do once they graduate. Franklin is thinking about a singing career with the Ensemble and he has discussed it with his finance' Arianna and she is on board with it. He simply thinks that as a group they can become a mighty force to be reckoned with. Their harmony and melody is out of this world. Johnny and Camille want to talk to Brenna as soon as possible because they think that they have a great chance at being recording artists. Someone had heard them sing in Syracuse and approached Johnny about the group and wanted to speak with the manager and Johnny told him that Brenna was the manager of their group. They wanted a business card from her and they took his name and phone number and told Mr. Charles Simmons that Brenna would be in touch with him. So as quickly as they all get settled from this trip, they need to table a general meeting with the Ensemble to get business cards printed up right away and get a tax ID number and the whole works to be paid legally. Somehow Brenna was working on this but had not sent the paper work off to Washington to form this Group of singers. She has to discuss with the group the official name that they are going to be using before she goes ahead with the paperwork. This has to be taken care of immediately so they can discuss with Kevin their name and bring up the subject of the CD and possibility of him going on tour.

The entire group has agreed on a name for the group. Shekinah Praise, this name kind of stood out for the group. We know we don't want it to be Kevin Snow and the Ensemble. This is out with the group. Most of them had already discussed this before they left for Syracuse, NY. They will work with Kevin on any project but they want to be independent of him. So, they have tabled a meeting in another week to discuss all particulars, since he has a manager already. If he wants to still be a part of the group its fine but they want to stay as a group not as background singers exclusively for Kevin. Brenna is thinking that maybe this might become an issue between the Ensemble and Kevin but she is keeping her fingers crossed. If they are going on tour with him for this CD it will be ok to be backgrounds singers but just for this tour. They also want to perform as a group together themselves. If the group is not busy it won't be a problem but when they are booked this could become a real problem for them. Brenna plans to be a professional manager for this group of singers as well as perform with them herself. If it becomes too much for her to manage the group and perform, she will hire someone else in the family to manage the group. Whatever she is a part of, she definitely wants James and his cousin Johnny to be a part of it as well as Julie. They have been together since they were eleven years old. If Julie's plans change when she gets married, we will deal with it then. Brenna got another Aha-moment, what if her two sisters and Julie's sister and brother can become background singers for

Kevin Snow. This would be awesome for them as well. Julie called her sister and brother about the idea and they liked it and Brenna's two sisters, Kim and Leah was excited when Brenna called them about the idea as well. Kevin was not too happy at first but he was willing to hear them as background singers for him. But he wanted the Ensemble to go on tour with him for his first CD because the Ensemble recorded with him and they had songs on the CD that he wanted everyone to hear when he goes on tour. This is great for the group.

The meeting is scheduled for the weekend coming up. Their meeting is tabled at the restaurant Carols in downtown Nashville. As they all gathered at the restaurant, they opened up the meeting with a word of prayer and then the meeting was in session. They all voted on the name Shekinah PRAISE. Kevin was ok with them not being background singers for him as long as they did the tour as background singer with him. He understood that they wanted to become a group all their own. He even liked the name the group picked out. His future wife is a part of this group and of course he's ok with it. He has told them that he wants them to be a part of his tour and they are really excited about this. Kevin doesn't have a problem with what the group wants in terms of them being their own separate entity. He also likes what Brenna is suggesting that her siblings can sing and also Julie's. They're all friends and this probably would be the plan for him as a solo artist with background singers. He knows they can sing from working with them during the Christmas concert. Everyone that Brenna has suggested have beautiful and strong voices. What Kevin is thinking of is taking the group with him as an opening act for him. He knows his future wife will be with the group and this would be good for him to be with or near her during this time when it may get a little hectic for him. Julie chimes in and say to the group that since they are all getting married to members of this group, it is a great idea and if there is a problem later on with the group, they just have to be sure they fulfill the contract before they can leave. No one can break their contract because then it becomes an issue. Brenna is thinking that with her and Julie running the studio and in charge of their contracts it won't be an issue. Once the contract is signed by all parties it's legal and binding. They know that Kevin's parents have entertainment lawyers to handle his business. The group however is just getting started with all legal forms being drawn up so they can become a gospel entity. They discussed everything from their side of the business to Kevin's side so everyone would be on the same page with out there being any surprises later on. As a group they tabled meetings every two weeks to get all ideas and future events on the table. Brenna and Julie are prioritizing everything so they can move forward. Everyone is amazed at how Brenna is handling all the particulars with little effort. She is also teaching Julie and Camille to join in and Arianna and Alice is working with the male attire. With all of them working so diligently they will have it all together when it's time for them to go on tour with Kevin.

After the meeting was over James and Brenna took in a movie to have some alone time with each other. Then they all met up at Franklin's apartment to just enjoy each other's company for a few hours. Alice and Terrence flew in for the meeting and now they are on their way back to Atlanta. Terrence likes the group so much that he is also thinking of joining them in one of the positions when Brenna opens up her studio with Julie. Some of the positions that they had discussed in the meeting he could certainly perform. The meeting was successful so they had some time to enjoy themselves and just go over a few songs to hear how they sounded with all their voices together except Alice.

The following week Kevin needed a meeting to discuss the tour attire. Cost will be picked up by him and his dad. After the discussion with them, Kevin tells them that over the next couple of months before his CD comes out and his tour begins, he wants their attire to be handled for the tour and they have a couple of months to do this. Kevin has hired a special person for wardrobe (personal shopper) and has picked out a day for them all to go and see what they think would look nice for performing. The wardrobe specialist/personal shopper will pick out the outfits and they will try them and see how well they look on the group. Now they are all excited about touring with a brand-new artist who is their personal friend. James, Johnny, and Franklin suggest for Shekinah Praise that they should wear all black for the opening act, ladies all black with pearls. During the next couple of months, they will decide their attire for the entire tour. With the group they will pick their own attire and book events around their last year of college.

Well it is time for Brenna and the rest of the group to take their finals for the end of the college semester. Everyone is rushing around to get to their classes and take their finals. Brenna has taken three and has three more to go and then she is done for the semester. She and Franklin has been studying together so they can ace their tests. After Brenna take her last three tests she will be packing for home. She needs a few weeks of rest and relaxation before the CD comes out and the tour begins. Brenna, Arianna and Franklin take their test and they are packed and ready to go home. James will be picking her up the very next day. What a whirlwind of a semester it had been for all of them.

None of them expected their career to take off like it did but it has and they are in another world. Brenna has taken care of everything to finalize their group and they are officially Shekinah Praise. She has gotten the contacts from Syracuse and they want them right away in Syracuse for a concert at Kevin's church and a few others in the surrounding areas. They planned on performing at Kevin church as a favor to Rev. Snow to show their gratitude to his parents that they really appreciate all he did for the group. Brenna has booked six events before the tour and will not book anymore until after the tour. This will be their first tour as a group and everyone is very excited. Their performance at Rev. Snow's church was fantastic and every one of their performances was so powerful. Every time the group performed, they seemed to become better and better singers. After the concert Shekinah Praise traveled back to Atlanta. After a few days, Brenna called the group in to discuss their finances and to let them know the cost of the tour. They cleared a good amount of revenue but there is still much to be done before they are financially stable as a group. They are now working on a CD of their own and it should be coming out in the spring of their last semester in college. Brenna and Julie's fathers told the girls that they had rented out a studio for them to record and they have been in the studio for the week working. What the girls don't know that this is their very own recording studio and it will not be revealed to the girls until their upcoming graduation.

Well it is time for them to go on tour with Kevin and they're all packed and ready to board his tour bus. They get to their first event and 'Shekinah Praise opened up for Kevin and they gave a superb opening performance. Then it was time for Kevin to come on and Julie stepped out and introduced him as a new artist because the event person had an emergency at the last minute and she automatically stepped in as Kevin explained it to her what was going on. James just loved Brenna even more and Kevin thought to himself what an exceptional person she is. He tells James later that she is a beautiful person and he has never seen a much nicer person in any one. He also thinks he got lucky himself because they are both friends with the same temperament. He loves Julie very much and wants them to always tour together and be around each other when they are traveling. He plans to talk to his parents about trying to check their bookings with each other. He knows this is going to be world war one with his parents since they are his managers. He knows that sometimes it will be totally impossible to keep them together because they are two separate entities. Kevin is also thinking of hiring Brenna as his manager as well and they could have all their bookings together. He thinks his parents are getting older and don't want on do all the traveling with him and especially keeping up with his booking and all the other things that go with it. He can still keep his entertainment lawyers as well and have them work with Brenna and Julie if they will agree to this. Kevin plans to talk to his parents about this to see what they think before he talks to Brenna. He doesn't want to make waves between the families because they all get along very well.

Johnny and Camille are looking at engagement rings and Camille is really serious right now and James seems to think Johnny is moving a little fast after he and Julie broke up. He has told Brenna about this and Brenna thinks Johnny needs to get over it because he was the one that wanted to break up with Julie. Julie is truly in love with Kevin now. James knows Johnny very well and know that he is not really over Julie. Camille has complained to him her concerns about Julie. She knows that Julie is not the problem it's Johnny. Well Brenna will talk to Julie about her feelings about Johnny to see if there is something still brewing with the two of them and if so they need to settle it before she gets married to Kevin.

CHAPTER
FOUR

I t is the middle of August and all the members of Shekinah Praise is all packed and ready to return to college. Brenda, Julie and the entire group is excited because for some of them, this is their last year of college and others are working on their masters (MBA). James and Brenna left early morning for Nashville. Julie, Kevin, Franklin and Arianna are leaving later on in the day. Alice has chosen to stay with her in-laws and finish up her degree in Florida. Her transferring to a different college in Atlanta will cause her to lose credits and she wants to stay on course for graduation in May. For when she comes home to Atlanta, she wants to be touring with Shekinah Praise and not worrying about college. If she goes back for her Masters, she will do on line classes and live in Atlanta with her husband and son.

Brenna and James arrived back at Vander Univ., where they picked up her dorm key and drove over to her dorm and moped and cleaned it completely. They put up curtains and placed all her items into the dorm room. James tells her that the dorm room is really looking great because of the hard work they've done. James tells her that the dorm room is really looking great because of all the work they've done. She has to go over to the storage to get her television, refrigerator and other appliances that she stored before coming home for the summer. James helped her get everything cleaned and sorted out before he leaves. He is so helpful to her and tells her all the time how much he loves and adores her. He hates to leave her because he won't see her until the end of September. He will see Brenna at their rehearsal for the Columbus Day event. He has double duty because he has yet to move into his apartment near his campus as well, but of course he will see that his love Brenna is set up before he leaves her. He is only an hour away but he has another day to get moved in. With him getting an apartment makes it much easier for him to get moved it. He has two more days to vacuum his place and get it all dusted and window treatments up and Bed mad up to his standard of living. His apartment is very modern and move in ready but he will clean it anyway. He loves being clean and neat. Johnny always tells him that he is a neat individual but its ok he just likes everything in place and everything looking great at all times. He tells Johnny when you keep it neat you can always find what you are looking for. Brenna's classes start in four days. She has registered on line for all her classes and got all that she needs for this semester by registering earlier. James left and moved into his apartment. He got settled pretty quickly and he's all set for his classes. They are well into their first semester of their fourth year of completing college and James is working on his MBA. Brenna has scheduled or rather tabled a meeting at a restaurant in James area. They are meeting at the restaurant to discuss the Thanksgiving and Christmas holidays back at home. Since she tells James everything, he cancelled the meeting at the restaurant and let them know that Brenna probably would be constantly calling to confirm everything. They promised to tell Brenna what she wants to hear about the meeting at the restaurant and things will continue to work out for the meeting. He has gotten the restaurant to cater for this event at his apartment. Brenna is not aware that the meeting has changed venues. Shekinah Praise has two events scheduled for October 14th and one November 12th, before they leave for the Thanksgiving holidays. These events are ticketed and contracts has already been signed and events must go on. Brenna will schedule an event around Martin Luther King's birthday the following year, but this event is free. Another event is scheduled for Black History month in February of the next years Semester which is five (5) months away. It is a charity event for one of the High schools in Nashville. They are giving back to the community. This will be their last charity event for a while as the group has gone professional. Their first CD will be out in a few months and they will begin their tour in June. Everyone will have graduated and all set to continue their career with Shekinah Praise except James. All the member of the group is so excited about their progress and know that it's all because of Brenna. James called and told Brenna that he loves her and counting down the hours and minutes until he sees her. She has updated him on all the events and she will bring this up in the meeting and get everyone on the same page. All the members can make the meeting except Alice and Terrence. They will conference in at the meeting. Alice and Terrence wants to fly in but a conference call will be ok unless they can take the time to travel to Nashville. We are not performing until the 14th of October, Columbus Day. Alice said that she is on fall break and she and Terrence will fly in to Nashville. Terrence have to fly to the corporate office of his company here in Nashville for a meeting. This will be perfect for the upcoming event. They will fly in for the November 12th Event as well. These events should bring in enough revenue to pay for their flights. Hopefully soon they will be set to start making money from their CD. They paid the coverage for the CD Cover Jacket and is waiting to get it in production and on the market as scheduled. This is a costly event but they have saved their own revenue for this and it is making a difference in the cost that would have set them back a great deal. Thanks to the business mine and sense of Brenna's Parents and siblings. Julie and Brenna will be great business partners. They had Tee Shirts made up and they are selling like hot cakes. This was the guy's idea, and Franklin has a business since he's been on campus selling Tees and they decided to have the Tees made up for these two events. This certainly will help them financially to get some of their expenses covered and have revenue left over.

Songs will be sent out on CD's so they will be ready for the performance. They are scheduling twelve (12) songs only to rehearse and have ready, only to perform no more than ten (10) of these songs. They always prepare more than what the concert is scheduled for because of the time frame of the concert and the event can run over or under. Their concert must go on even if they have to pull other songs out of their repertoire. The meeting is tabled two days away and Brenna is making sure that everything is in place and ready to be discussed. Brenna asked everyone to think about some of the things they want to discuss and write down the questions so they can move through the meeting quickly. She will be riding up with Franklin and Arianna for the meeting. James tells Franklin what he has done but did not share it with the girls. They are on their way to James and Franklin drives them straight up to James Apartment. They are all out of the care and in James apartment and it is really nice and spacious. Everything is all set up and they have hosts from the Restaurant to serve them. The dining room is all set up for them like a conference room to start their meeting. Brenna is smiling and so thankful that James and the fellas surprised them with this luncheon. Its makes it even special for them because they can discuss in private their affairs without being in a restaurant where their business may be heard. James proceeded to tell them that the meeting will be at the apartment instead of the restaurant. He couldn't see how they could have a productive meeting at a restaurant especially since they needed to do a conference call to Alice & Terrence this weekend. Terrence traveled to Florida this weekend to be with Alice for the conference from his parent's home either by phone or computer. He traveled the night before so he would be there for this conference. Shekinah Praise agreed on their scheduled dates and they are set for their performances. Everything was brought out and discussed about the dates of releasing their CD and touring right after graduation. The meeting was two hours and fifty minutes. James, Kevin, Johnny and Franklin had the food catered and it was like a party for them. They played their CD after the caterers left to be on the safe side and it sounded great. The pronunciation of their words was clear on the CD and it was just a great day for them. They continued to sit around and occasionally singing together. Kevin asked Brenna to perform the song that Terrence wrote for Alice. Brenna sang the song with so much soul, spirit and joy and Kevin thought to himself what can't she do. She did an outstanding job on the song. They want to start practicing songs that other leaders sing in case of emergencies that may occur when performances have to go on. Brenna, Arianna and Julie think this is a great idea and will table another meeting to share it with other members of Shekinah Praise. They hope Alice is in favor of this as well because there are other songs that they want to work with her on as well. This is a way of cross training each member to work and minister to audiences when there is a crisis/emergency with a member (s.) They are training to be one of a kind in Gospel singing. They don't want to be just contemporary singers; they want to be able to sing to any audience. God has blessed them with their great gift of voices and they want to be able to use them and bless their audiences with it.

James is trying to get Brenna's attention so they can close out and go out on their date night. She turns and see him calling out to her. They close the meeting with a prayer and it time for everyone to leave. Franklin took Arianna and left for his apartment. The catering people has closed down their services and left and now it's just James, Brenna, Julie and Kevin. James tells her what a great evening it was and gives her the biggest kiss ever. Kevin is holding Julie and they are going along to the movies with James and Brenna. It was a great evening and now they want to go to the movies. Brenna is still worried about Johnny and his feelings toward Julie. He seemed a little quieter tonight although Camille was with him and he just didn't seem like himself. Brenna noticed that he was smiling when he was near Julie but the minute, he left her side and he came near Camille his smile left his face completely. They left first and was headed back to Johnny's apartment near Camille's dorm. Brenna hopes that he is not still in love with Julie because Julie is completely smitten with Kevin. She plans to talk to him soon about it to see if he will open up and say what's on his mind. He was the one that broke off their relationship and now it may be too late to salvage it. Julie seems to be extremely happy with Kevin. She thought Johnny was moving too fast with getting out of their relationship but who was she to question them about their relationship and what they were doing.

Kevin tells Brenna that he still wants to perform with the group until he has to go on tour for himself. He's hoping that they will continue to be his opening act for his next tour and to introduce them as the next group of performers that has gone professional and will be introducing their new CD in the spring. They will have an option or some kind of stipulation to sing with each other or not to perform together. The group includes the original ten members, and nine if Kevin goes completely solo. His future wife Julie will remain a member of Shekinah Praise and an integral business partner to Brenna. They have been friends so long and they seem more like sisters than friends. The details of Kevin remaining will be worked out by the lawyers from Atlanta, GA and Syracuse, NY. Brenna has contacted and acquired entertainment lawyers. The lawyers has been in contact with one another and everything is moving smoothly. When she was looking for lawyers she sought out artist that has been in the gospel industry for a while and was given great advice on the lawyers that she had acquired. She felt really great about the team of Lawyers that will be representing Shekinah Praise. The lawyers from Atlanta know the lawyers from Syracuse very well because they are in the same business. Kevin cannot be contracted by two entities at the same time. If he is or has promised to do three or four CD's for his father's studio, he has to complete his obligation there before he can do anything with Shekinah Praise. He will have to make a decision on this pretty quickly because as a professional group they are ready to move on with their business deals and contracts. They can do back up singing for Kevin but cannot be on contract with his team. Brenna has taken care to contact her siblings to do background singing for Kevin as well as Julie's sibling. Shekinah Praise will be working out of their own studio as soon as Brenna and Julie graduates. Brenna has called several places for empty buildings to be bought and renovated within a couple of months of their graduations. One place in particular answered their call and with a good price and Brenna asked them if they would be interested in renovating the building for them in May or June if they purchase the building in April. The owner already knew who Julie was when she put the call into them. The girls are still not aware that their parents has already purchased a building and it is the same building that's being renovated while they are finishing up their degree. Brenna has made up her mind that she and Julie needed to talk to their parents about purchasing the building and getting it renovated for them. They are told that the building needed to be brought up to code before they can rent it or make a sale. This is fine with Julie and Brenna as they won't need it until they graduate in May.

Now that they're all back at their apartments and respective dorms, it's time for Shekinah Praise to get ready for their classes before Columbus Day event. As a reminder, Julie called Brenna to let her know that she and Kevin would be arriving down at her dorm to go over their songs for Columbus Day. James has already arrived because it's their date night and they will be hanging out together with Franklin and Arianna later on. Their date is still on but they cannot stay out to late because Brenna has a term paper that she is working on and a quiz she has to study for in two days. She has to keep up with her class work as well. When it's time for graduation, she doesn't want any surprises at the last minute popping up. Johnny and Camille is arriving shortly while Alice and Terrence is being conferenced in via computer so they can see and hear all the songs and practice along with the members of the group. After graduation their permanent home will be Atlanta and it will be much easier to have their practice at their own facility. Since going professional before their graduation is extremely hard on the entire group. It's an awesome task with class work and sometime performing but they are willing to stay the course. Brenna and Julie has limited their events out of state until they can travel freely without worrying about anything except the business at hand with Shekinah Praise. Brenna is worried that they will be losing money but they are committed to getting their degree. They will look into purchasing transportation for Shekinah Praise once they are well established. This will be handled through the business. They don't won't to purchase everything too fast and then go bankrupt.

Now they all have gathered in the theater at Vander University rehearsing for their Columbus Day event. Their rehearsal went very well and they rehearsed all their songs. As they are getting ready to leave the director of the theater Mr. Michael Brice approached Brenna and asked if they would consider doing a concert on Campus in March. She tells Mr. Brice that she will discuss with Shekinah Praise and get back to him within the next day. As this is her university that has done so much for her Franklin and Arianna, however she doesn't think it will be a problem to do it but she don't want to agree to it until she check with everyone that is involved with Shekinah Praise. She herself is willing to do this free for the University but the lawyers may think differently about it although she is the manager she still ask for advice from her lawyers. As Mr. Brice walks away he is thinking to himself, what can he do to help his students that has been so dedicated in his class of music? He did hear them performing and had been out in the back of the theater listening. He will have to think of something. They really are that good and he is so proud that members from his music class is a part of this professional group. Brenna talked to the members and they all thought it was a great idea to do the concert and insisted on it being a free concert for all the students from the different colleges that they all are attending. Brenna will give Mr. Brice the names of the colleges and see if they would like to attend the concert. They will do the concert for Friday, Saturday and Sunday. They will advertise and get all flyers out in the community. Mr. Brice has given his word for Brenna, Arianna, and Franklin that their performance will be a portion of their grade. Each one has to perform individually for this to work for their grade. It is mandatory that All the Musical theater directors from the different colleges be present to grade their students on their performances. Mr. Brice talked to the musical directors from the colleges and some of them agreed and some of them did not agree. But they were willing to come down and see the concert to actually see and evaluate their student performances. Maybe this could be something that the colleges could get together and do at the end of their college year for their seniors who are graduating and moving on in the musical industry. None of them had ever thought of this before but it was an interesting thought for them to consider in the future of the colleges. Especially if their musical theater department is made up of a small group of musical performers. The four colleges could merge their plays and do several performances at each college and run them for a week during their senior year. These plays could be ticketed events to help each college musical theater department. But all of these things are on the back burner until they can get through the Columbus Day event.

Now their rehearsal is over and they are on their date night at the movies and Brenna is just so happy to be in James arms as they have not seen each other in a few weeks. Julie is talking to Kevin and seems like something is wrong but Brenna doesn't know what it is. She noticed the same thing with Johnny and Camille but she is hoping that everything is ok in paradise. They make a great couple but its better they find it out now than later when they are married. As they left the theater everyone is happy and embracing each other and Brenna is thinking to herself that whatever it was with Julie and Kevin they must have worked it out. She will talk to Julie later on tonight. Later on that night Julie called Brenna before she called her. Brenna asked her was something wrong with her and Kevin and she said yes but it had been settled. It seems that Camille had gotten upset at her about Johnny and she was surprised to know that she was so upset at her. Camille thought that Johnny was paying more attention to Julie than her and this became a problem for her and she spoke to Kevin about it. Kevin asked Julie if there was something going on with her and Johnny because he knew they use to be an item. Julie became annoyed at Kevin because she is wearing his ring and nothing is coming between them at this point as she loves Kevin very much. What she and Johnny had is over and she has moved on with Kevin. Camille needs to do the same thing with Johnny. Now Brenna is wondering if this is going to be an ongoing problem with the two of them in Shekinah Praise. They need to get together and get this ironed out before it becomes a problem. Going forward they don't need to take problems into the group. Camille called Julie the very next day to inquire if she and Johnny was seeing each other again and of course Julie was a little on the offensive side. She let Camille know that she has nothing to worry about when it comes to her because she is very much in love with her future husband Kevin and she wanted to know where she got the idea that she was back together with Johnny. They have not been together in two years. They kind of fell out of love with each other and it was more Johnny's choice to move on. Julie said to Camille that it hurt for a while but she got over it and kept Christ at the center of her life when this happen and then she met a great guy in Kevin. Johnny maybe stepping out on Camille with someone else but it sure is not her. And again Johnny maybe trying to make Camille jealous for whatever reason. They settled things between themselves and Camille apologized to Julie and said maybe she read something into what was always friendship between the two and hopefully this will be the end of that discussion. Concert day is here and they are rushing around on the stage with sound check and making sure that everything will go off perfect. This is a ticketed event and it must be great out there for their audience. They will not let their audiences down as they have gone professional and this is more like show casing their talent before their CD comes out. Everything they do within the next five to seven months on stage must be perfected. Well the Events MC came out and introduced himself and then the artist for the evening. They were called by their professional name Shekinah Praise and as the latest artist that will be hitting the charts pretty soon and Brenna hit the stage and took the MIC and it was a night they will never forget their very first concert as professional singers. Her very first song was just perfect without any flaws. Brenna spoke briefly to the audience and introduced Julie as the next singer and Julie brought the house down, and after that Terrence and Alice sang a duet which was just great. Then it was time for Kevin to sing and boy did he do a great job. He is just phenomenal once he hits the stage. Johnny and Camille sang a duet and then it was time that James express to the audience the love he has for Christ Jesus and all that he brought him through with losing his mom and dad at a very young age and meeting the love of his life at thirteen years old, his future wife Brenna. He told the audience they have known each other most of their lives and he knew she was the one for him at that age. She showed him how to live a Christian life and still enjoy life as a teenager. They sang together in church and they are still singing and serving God together. Then James and Brenna sang their song together from their childhood church, and they still remember the song although they rearranged it and sang it their way and they were awesome together. Brenna thanked the audience and asked Kevin to come and sing with her and they brought the house down. Brenna got so happy that she could hardly contain herself. This was the second time that the group had ever seen Brenna sing with so much power, joy and spirit. This song they sang in Syracuse and it was added on his CD because they liked it so well and it was executed to perfection. They went on break for fifteen minutes and then back on stage for another fifteen minutes and what a great audience and great concert as well. They were well pleased with having a packed out house and selling all their Tee Shirts. This was one of the greatest concerts that Shekinah Praise ever performed together with their new name. So many Booking Agents wanted to book them right away but they have to push the dates out to the next year because they don't won't to overbook and then they can't meet the requirement dates because they have classes and this would not look good for them in the future. They must graduate on time so they can pursue their career. How is Brenna going to handle the Agents is very simple to her, she will write the number in sequence on their business card and this will be how she handle who gets the concert first. The Venue will play a major part in this as well. This was explained to all the Agents and they understood but wanted to hurry and get them booked ASAP. As they talked to each one she listed them by their card number on her computer with their information and phone number. This concert really put them on the map and they cannot believe the concert hall was sold out and their November 12th concert is almost sold out as well. With them doing so well maybe they will schedule another concert in Atlanta the beginning of December. This is not a long drive from Nashville and they might rent the Limo to bring them down for this concert. They have some equipment back at home or they can rent what they need. Normally the Concert halls provide the musical equipment for the artist. They will discuss this concert within a few days. They have an event person that want them to do a concert in December but Brenna had turn them down. She will get back on the phone to let them know that they can do the concert for them. But after this one they won't be available to do another until they graduate. Brenna is in a play for the college in April and cannot book the group until the play is finished. The play normally runs for a week at Vander University.

As Shekinah Praise is leaving the venue, they are on such a high that the concert finished on a great note and no glitches for them and their music was on Que. After everyone were all packed up to leave, they prayed to their Heavenly Father for letting them have such a great concert and the Limousine took them back to their hotel. What a great night they all had. None of them could linger too long because they are exhausted and need to rest themselves and their voices. After they returned to the hotel the manager gave them one of their ballrooms for socializing with some of their friends and some of the Agents but they kept it on a small scale to keep it in control. They are Christians and they want to continue to serve the Lord as they always have and remain truthful to Him. God is an awesome God just trust him and let him use you. There was more artist there at the concert and they were invited back to the hotel as well to celebrate with them as new artist. The hotel did an outstanding job of hosting them there as new artists. Their ballroom was decorated just for them and they had tee shirts, key chains, booklets and pictures on display. The Tee shirts were selling like hot cakes and they thought they were going to run out. Franklin had other Tees in his hotel room that could be brought to the ballroom if they needed more. Brenna had invited her musical director from the college and the students came out in great numbers to support them at the event. They were blessed beyond measure.

The next morning, they were on cloud nine and everyone that saw them wanted an autograph. This was a great feeling for them as a new artist and they were basting in its glory. They were checking out of the hotel in another day so they had time to rehearse some of the songs they were going to perform on November 12th. All the fellows were going to check on equipment that they will need to travel with and start purchasing a few pieces at a time so when they get ready to go on tour they will have all their equipment in place and paid for. James came up to Brenna and wanted her to go with him to dinner. Brenna and James went out to their favorite restaurant and had dinner. James just wanted some alone time to see her and hold and kiss her for a while since they don't get a lot of time for socializing. James and Brenna have almost another year before they will be married and it gets harder and harder to wait for their marriage but they made a promise to each other. Both of them even went to the shopping mall to purchase a few items for themselves before they went back to the hotel. It seems like everyone had the same idea they had, because no one was at the hotel when they got back. So they did a few lapses in the pool and remained there until the entire group came out and got in the pool as well. They had an awesome time with each other. Johnny and Camille are much happier as Brenna watch their reaction toward each other. Whatever it was they seemed to have worked it out. Terrence and Alice came over to Brenna and James and she is so happy that she had been include in the group to perform with them. She talked to Brenna and told her that this was something she wanted to do all along and did not know how to talk to them because of her attitude with her in high school. Brenna found out that Alice is a nice person when you just give her a chance, however Shekinah Praise did give her that chance and now they're all great friends and moving on. After they left, James said to Brenna that Terrence is a great guy and is the right person to handle Alice. Kevin and Julie walked over and they had a great conversation about the group and what they see in the future for the group. Do you think that everyone will remain with the group long term? This was the question that Kevin asked and Brenna seems to think so unless they want to go solo and this will change the group completely unless some of their family members can fill in. Everyone in Shekinah Praise are from families with natural born abilities in singing. What a joy everybody sings. Kevin wants to start his family in two years and Brenna thinks this is a great idea as well because they will be on maternity leave at the same time and back with the group in a few months to tour again. Since their parents still live in the surburbs of Atlanta they will no doubt have baby sitters. But this conversation can be discussed at a later date because no one is married yet and has not been discussed with their fiancé's. It is time for them to start putting together the songs for their event coming up November 12th, in two weeks. After their rehearsal tonight the limo will drop everyone off that is on campuses in Nashville on tomorrow.

They are back in their dorms on campus and Brenna has a quiz on Monday. Following Monday Brenna aced the test because she studied for it. She had a real busy week with the rest of her classes and the play. One week to go and then the next event, although Brenna is in a play that will be presented this week has really exhausted her to near breaking point. The play will run Monday, Tuesday and Wednesday. Mr. Brice is working with her so she can get all her grades for this semester, but the play must go on this week with Brenna, Arianna and Franklin. They will have Thursday and Friday to practice on their songs for the concert. All is well with the songs they will be presenting because they rehearsed them for the Columbus Day event and during the week after. To hear them one only has to guess that they stay prayed up because their concerts are flawless. The play was presented without any incidents and they have two days to rest and get together for Saturday night's concert for Shekinah Praise. The concert was beautiful and executed so well. They took their concert to another level and every one was on a spiritual high. James had to sit Brenna down at one point because she was so emotional. She gets spiritually high when she sings for the Lord. For her this is only God working through her. Kevin took over and they all finished on such a high note. Great Concert for them and they got a standing ovation for this concert. Most of them were so exhausted but they took the time to sign autographs for the audience. What a blessing and an honor to do this. They will never forget where their blessings come from. Now they will rest for a few days before they get ready to go home to Atlanta. They will do the Thanksgiving holiday again but on a smaller scale or rather they think they will do it on a smaller scale.

James calls Brenna and Franklin to see when everyone will be ready to travel back to Atlanta for the holidays. She just can't wait to see her parents although they came up to their very first concert as professionals in Nashville, TN. All Shekinah Praise can say is their parents really supports them in all they do.

CHAPTER
FIVE

What a weekend of Concerts and plays for Brenna and two of her classmates. They made it through their toughest week ever. Shekinah Praise has now traveled back home to Atlanta for the Thanksgiving Holidays. Brenna says to her mom that she is exhausted and that this last year for her and the group has been very taxing and she don't know how much time she'll have to get the studio renovated and ready for the group to start their recording. But her mom tells her that it will work itself out. She did not break her promise to her husband by telling Brenna that the studio will be ready for them once they graduate college. Her mom and dad as well as the parents of Julie will take them to the renovated studio that has been purchased for both girls and will give them the keys to the building. Brenna says ok to her mom after she says that it will work itself out and she knows that she has so much work to do since she is the manager of the group Shekinah Praise. Brenna calls Julie to see if she has an hour to go over a few details for Thanksgiving and get their program lined up for the church. They have to go over to meet Paster Derrick Hoffman to see what the church schedule is like. Rev Derrick is in the office and motion for them to come in. He gives them the program that his assistant has scheduled out for the Thanksgiving Eve service. He left room for them to make adjustments for the songs that Shekinah Praise will be Performing. The administrative assistant has already added their choir and Brenna lets her know that they only plan to do not more than three songs unless the Holy Spirit leads them to continue on in praise. They are just so exhausted from the previous two concerts in Nashville and the play at the college. Shekinah Praise will meet tomorrow morning and go over the three songs for the service. The following morning all is present at the church making sure the music is spot on for their songs and the songs for the choir. The choir joined them with their rehearsals as well. They don't anticipate doing a concert tonight just the three songs for the service. Pastor Derrick is so proud of them and loves it when they come home and do the service for him. He must tell all his friends because the church is always packed when they get there. He enjoys telling the story of this group of kids growing up in his church and going on to college and coming home and not forgetting where they came from.

Brenna and Julie tell Terrance and Alice that they will be singing their song and Johnny and Camille as well tonight. The pastor has been in the present of most of them singing but he has not heard the new members and Terrence and Alice will get to show case their talent as well. It's now Thanksgiving Eve and the church is filled to capacity for the service. The Gospel praise group is ready to hit the sanctuary for the worship and praise. After the worship and praise was done, Pastor prays and sets the tone for the service and then calls on the choir to sing. They sang so beautifully together with great Spirit and Power. They asked Shekinah praise to join in with them. As Pastor Derrick was speaking softly, he asked a request of Brenna to sing his favorite song for him and she brought the house down. Pastor Derrick loves to hear Brenna sing even from a very young girl. He wanted Shekinah Praise to give them two selections and two after the gospel has been preached. Terrence and Alice sang their song and it was just awesome. Johnny and Camille came out of their shell and stunned the Congregation with the song they performed. Pastor Derrick stood up and said I have never heard such beautiful music and songs coming from my children of this church. He was so happy that Johnny and his Finance' showed his side of talent as well. Then Pastor Derrick preached one of the most powerful messages that Brenna has ever heard him do and sang a song as well. Kevin and Julie poured out their hearts with their song and then James and Brenna completed it with their song. They took it to another level and everyone in the church was on their feet shouting and just praising God to the highest. Pastor Derrick asked Shekinah Praise to come up and have a word with the congregation about their group going professional. Pastor had then all to say a few words of encouragement to other singers in the congratulation to let them know that it can be done again if they just keep on singing and trusting in the Lord and sit back and watch what God will do in your life. Now it was time for Brenna to explain to the congregation that they had formed the group right here in this church and named the group Shekinah Praise. Brenna also told them that they already have so many Events already scheduled right now that they have to put it on hold until after graduation. They have to focus on their class work and then they can start booking events and completing their CD by April 1st, so it can be on the market by early June. Brenna let the congregation know that they would not be where they are today without the support of the church and their many friends and colleagues there in Atlanta. James steps up and tells the Pastor that they will send down some of their CD's to the church when they are out of production. Brenna tells pastor that he will get the first one. She smiles and tells pastor that the service is back in his hands. He motions for Brenna to sing and she nods her head and thanks the church again and she turns to Franklin and Arianna to close them out with a song. The service was beautiful and they basically kept to their schedule because they are exhausted. Pastor thanks them and tells everyone to have a happy Thanksgiving and to travel home safely. As they join the members out in the vestibule, they decided among themselves that they will go home early and get some rest because each one of them are truly tired. All their parents came for the service to hear their children as professionals in their home town of Atlanta. The Press in Atlanta has been all over them since they found out about them being brand new gospel artist. It really made the entire group feel really special and they can hardly contain themselves. It's a great feeling and a Blessing for them. Julie and Brenna look at each other and say I think we are almost there but there is plenty more work to be done before they will have it all together and ready to go on tour. There is the matter of them opening up their own studio which Brenna and Julie will be handling real soon.

They returned home after church and James decides to spend some time with his girl Brenna at her home. They spent time in the kitchen with her mother as she is preparing a dish for Thanksgiving Dinner. Brenna tells James that her mom makes a pretty mean dinner for Thanksgiving as if you don't know and he laughs and sneaks a kiss while her mom has her back turned away. Mrs. Smaller is smiling too herself because she's remembering when she and George were young and stealing a kiss whenever they thought no one was looking. Out of the corner of her eye she sees James kissing Brenna. She turns around and they both blush because they just got caught. He smiles and tells Mrs. Smaller he couldn't help himself. She smiles and tells them its ok and she is not going to stand in the way of love. Her two sisters and their husbands, Kim and Charles Walker and Leah and husband Michael Henderson, are here to help Mom prepare dinner for Thanksgiving. They came over after service with their contribution in their cars. Ivan called earlier to let mom know he would be over tomorrow for dinner with his girlfriend. James greets everyone and let them know that he's on his way home. Brenna walks him to the door and he plants a kiss on her that leaves her shivering in her shoes. All she could say was WOW and he tells her how much he loves and adore her. Well Mr. Williams the feeling is mutual. About an hour after he left, Julie calls Brenna and let her know that Kevin is flying out Thanksgiving morning for Syracuse, NY to spend the Thanksgiving Holiday with his parents this year. She tells Brenna that she is flying out at 5:00 early Friday morning to be with him and go shopping for their parents for Christmas. She tells Brenna that she will arrive in Syracuse at 10:30 AM. They will shop after they leave the airport so they won't have to come back downtown again. Brenna tells her to enjoy herself and she will see her at Christmas. Brenna checks up on Johnny and Camille and they are spending Thanksgiving at her parent's home and having dessert at Johnny's grandparents. As she is talking to Camille and Johnny, Brenna hears the doorbell ring and its Franklin and Arianna stopping over to see her. Their plans are to spend Thanksgiving dinner at her parent's home and they are going to Franklin's for coffee and dessert.

Alice has been flying home to Atlanta on the weekends to get the house in order. While Terrence was home, he hired some of his coworkers and some of Alice's family to help him get all the furniture in place in the house and with Alice flying in and driving in sometime to get things in place for the Thanksgiving Holiday. She has settled into her new home and her in-laws are there to make dinner for her and Terrence because they know the two of them are literally exhausted from the previous concerts and service that evening at church. This is his parent's very first time at their new home in Atlanta. Mrs Black has prepared most of the dinner already and they will be there with Terrence, and the baby for a few weeks. Alice's mom has agreed to watch Terrence Jr., while Alice complete her final semester in Florida. She has a few more months in Florida and she will be back in Atlanta permanently with her husband and son along with her family when she graduates.

Her in-laws are looking for a house in the Atlanta area. They have set up appointment with the realtor to go out again the following week. There was one house that they liked and the realtor said that they have a very good chance to get the house. Their house is on the market back in Florida and as soon as it sells, they hope to have purchased a home here in Atlanta to be close to their son, his wife and grandson.

Well Shekinah Praise have Friday and Saturday to enjoy their families because they will be traveling back to school on Sunday. James and Brenna went Christmas shopping for their Parents on Friday so when they return home for Christmas most of their shopping will be done and they can spend quality time with each other. They got most of their gifts with only a couple left to get when they return home. On Saturday they will meet up at Alice and Terrence to see if they can help out for a few hours. They had all called each other and Brenna called Alice to see if they were going to be home and if it was ok to come over for a while to help them out. They welcomed all of them to come over. When they arrived there, Alice had very thing in place and the house was completely furnished and looking great. Alice explained that she had been coming home on the weekend to get her home in live in condition. She laughs and said it took a while but with the help of her family, friends and Terrence co-workers they were able to get it done rather quickly. Terrence and Alice welcomed the entire group into their home. What a lovely home that she and Terrence owned. Julie and Brenna saw that they did not need their help in the way of placing things into place in their home as they have done so already. Shekinah Praise only stayed a couple of hours but Alice seems happier now that we are all friends and Terrence is more open with suggestions concerning the group and is willing to help put together any Event that they have.

Brenna is watching how well he is working out with the group and want to talk to Julie and Alice about Terrence working as their Public Relations Person for them. He has a great business mine and this is basically what they need in the group. Now that the work load is getting a little hectic for Brenna and Julie, they are going to consider hiring a manager to handle everything for them. Julie thinks that Brenna should remain the manager and they bring in Terrence as an assistant until they get to know him a little better. They will discuss this when they get back to their dorms and have their first meeting. Shekinah Praise has grown to ten people now and they have to start handling things as a business. Julie thinks that James can help Brenna as the manager and they will be fine. Brenna doesn't want the group to start thinking that it's all about Julie, Brenna and James. They want to add to the group from within so there will be a balance there. Either Franklin, Johnny or maybe even Kevin. Julie don't want to put anything else on Kevin because he is looking at a Solo career in the Gospel Industry. He needs people to help him out and has already asked Brenna to step in and manage him as well. She can manage both with help. If they are performing in different directions this will become a problem for her but if they have two managers working together or if they are a husband and wife team, it can be done especially with the group being as close to Kevin and sometime performing with him and his future wife who is a member of Shekinah Praise.

Brenna had introduced her parents to Terrence parents at the church some time ago. They did not know each other a they lived in Florida and even Alice's parents did not know her parents very well but all of that has changed now since the girls have become close friends and in a professional group together.

Well James and Brenna left Alice's house on a good note and they're on their way home as Brenna and James, want to get an early start tomorrow morning with their Christmas shopping for their parent. They were all piling into their cars at the same time going home. James pauses in his car and puts his arms around Brenna and tells her he is so in love with her and can't wait to be married in six and a half months. He kisses her with all the passion that he has for her. She just melts in his arms and tells James she loves him too. Julie left and went straight to her parents as she is leaving very early tomorrow morning for Syracuse New York.

James and Brenna are up early to go shopping for the Christmas holidays for their parents. When you go early on Friday mornings after Thanksgiving you catch some awesome sales and deals. Brenna has two nieces and two nephews to buy for and she want to get it out of the way early and wrap it for her mom and dad to put under the Christmas tree. James picks out gifts for his grandparents and his sister and three cousins. Johnny's eldest sister has gotten married and is expecting her first baby. So just gifts for her little one and something smart for her. James says she wants to get herself a tablet and we stopped at AT&T to purchase her one and have it wrapped. The husband is easy to buy for. Johnny calls while they are out shopping and want to meet up down town Atlanta. They meet at the Atlanta Pulp restaurant for lunch. Johnny and Camille has lots of gifts that they have purchased in the trunk of their car and so does James and Brenna. She will shop in Nashville for James because he is with her every second and she can't get him anything with him in tow. Johnny and Camille pay for their lunch and they are just enjoying themselves when one of their old friends Brett, walks in and join them for lunch with his girlfriend Emily. They really have a nice time talking to them. They asked if it was true that they have gone professional and they were so happy to tell them that it is true and that their CD would be coming out in late spring. Brenna always liked Brett when they were in high school. He was just a nice all-around person and everyone liked him. He is an associate pastor in one of the churches downtown Atlanta. They were surprised to hear of this and wants to come and visit his church the next time they are home. He loves to hear this and wants them to come down and let him introduce them to the congregation at his church. They liked the idea because this could turn into something big for them. Brenna's mother told her never turn down the hand that may one day feed you so she always remembers her mother's words. Brett told them that he would be getting married in June and if they are home, they will be getting an invitation from them. Brenna told Brett that she and James is getting married the first weekend in July. She told Brett to mail the invitation to her parent's home as they would be home late May. They finished lunch and thanked Brett for inviting them to his church and they went their separate ways.

On Saturday morning Brenna will take her mom out to get something for her dad and will get her a nice necklace and earrings to math in Nashville when she gets back to college. With all bases covered James brings her home and he drives home to spend some quality time with his family but not before making plans for Brenna and himself for Saturday evening. James spent an hour with Brenna at her home. He tells Brenna that he loves her and kisses her like he couldn't get enough of kissing her. She just loves this side of James because he is so sweet, kind and gentle to her. He gets up and tells her he is leaving before he embarrasses himself and she understood what he meant. She walked him to the door and give him another kiss and she closes the door.

Brenna walks into the sitting room with her mom and dad and her mom asked her what was wrong because she had such a down look on her face and she tell her mom that she just loves him so much. Mom tells Brenna that she understands because she loved her dad the same way and still does. They know what each other are saying even before it is said. That's love girl and she explained to Brenna that she sees much of herself in her and that is something she should be very proud of. Her mom makes it so easy to talk to and she takes advantage of it all. Dad says to Brenna that he is so proud of her and continue to be a young lady that any man would be proud to call her his wife. She understands what her dad is saying without him saying it directly. He gets up and comes over to Brenna and give her a big hug before he tells her mom that he is going to bed so they can have a talk. Her dad understands her so well too. He knew that she wanted to talk to her mom. Brenna tells her mom that it is getting so hard to wait until marriage but they both made a promise that they would stay celibate until they get married. Mom looks at Brenna and tells her that's my girl and stick to your promise because she only has six more months. She had waited this long she can wait another six months. She knows she will because when they get back to college, they will be so busy with studying for their finals before they come back for the Christmas Holidays. She tells her mom that she needs to talk to Julie but don't know if she and Kevin are home or not and her mom tells her you won't know unless you call her and see. That's all Brenna wanted to hear and she picked up the phone and dialed her number and her mom came over and gave her a hug and told her good night and would talk to her tomorrow morning. Kevin answered her phone and said that Julie just went upstairs for a minute and would be right back down in a few moments. He asked Brenna how she and James was doing and she said wonderful. As they are talking about James Julie walked back into the room and she said that's Brenna and he answered yes. Ok Brenna I will go and talk to my parents a few minutes and you can catch Julie up on plans. They were so busy discussing their upcoming wedding and saying how much they are in love with their finance's and how hard it's getting to wait until they are married. Julie is letting Brenna know that it's almost unbearable but they must be truthful to who they are. They both know they are great girls and hope the guys appreciate them for waiting until they are married before sharing a bed with them. After they finished their conversation, Brenna tells Julie that she will see her the week they do the concert in Nashville on January 15th. Julie and Kevin will be flying back to Nashville because Kevin's brother will drive the car back from Atlanta for them. Kevin and Julie will shop on Saturday and fly back to Nashville on Sunday morning to start preparing for their finals.

So, Brenna is thinking to herself that they will start with the Christmas Holidays of being back at home. They will go to church and the choir will do their Christmas concert and they will remain seated in the sanctuary unless called upon to sing a solo or something. More than likely the church will understand that they are preparing now for their January 15th, concert when they get back to Nashville as well as the Black history month concert. She plans to call Pastor Derrick Hoffman and inform him that they won't be performing this holiday but will sing a couple of songs for the Holidays if he prefers them too. A few of the members of Shekinah Praise will be out of town for the holidays and won't be able to perform with them. So, they will do a couple of songs just Brenna, Julie, James and Johnny. Her mine is racing with different thoughts of how they're going to handle the upcoming Christmas Holidays and prepare for the January 15th concert.

Well she finished up her conversation with her mother and she tells her mom that she is going to bed because she wants to take her shopping the first thing in the morning for her day and then hang out with James later. It's Saturday morning and Brenna and her mom is down town Atlanta and they get all their shopping done and they ran into James, Johnny and their grandparents. They were shopping as well and they talked briefly and agreed to meet in a few hours. Later on, that afternoon James, picks up Brenna at her home and they go out to dinner and then to a nice club. They don't frequent the club scene often but sometime they will go out with a few friends that's home from college and just have a great time with them. It's getting late and James ask Brenna if she is ready to leave and of course she says yes because they will have to leave tomorrow around 8:30 AM to get back to their dorms and be ready for class on Monday morning.

Julie, Brenna and all their friends arrive back in Nashville from their Thanksgiving Holiday and others to towns farther north to their dorms to prepare for their finals. After the first two weeks she is going to her first final and she need to aced this test because she thinks this is the hardest test for her. As she is well into the test, she discovered that she is more than prepared for this test and it was not that bad. She went on to finish all her test and was waiting for them to post the grades for all the students to see. She got all A's on all her test and she was beyond overjoyed. Now she can start preparing for the trip back home to Atlanta for the Christmas holidays. She can't wait to tell her parents the goods news of her finals. James also did well and he was very pleased with himself as well. He only feared one class which was his math class and he got an A- in that class which made him very happy. Franklin and Arianna got good grades as well and everyone seems to be just overjoyed over what they have accomplished this semester. Well she has gone back to her dorm and got her clothes together for driving home with James and this is a few hours for them to get home. Boy she hates traveling but they have to get home for Christmas.

Now they are all packed and ready to travel home for the holidays. The weather seemed to be a bit colder and she needs to find her boots, gloves and hat for the trip home. Brenna's mine is constantly wondering how they are going to get everything done for the concert in January and the one for Black History month in Nashville. As Brenna and James are on their way home, they stop and get snack food for the trip. They don't eat heavy meals before they travel. It makes them tired and sleepy. James always tell Brenna that she eats like a bird anyway but Brenna just like keeping fit and staying in shape and looking nice for her boo. She wants her clothes to fit her perfect when she puts them on. James and Brenna had only made a couple of stops and now they are approaching the Atlanta Area and Brenna is tired and just want to get home to her parents and take a nap. When they arrived to her parents and pull up in the drive way all of her siblings are there and immediately, she sensed something was not right and wanted to know what was wrong. Well she goes inside with James in tow with her and her dad is there with his PJ'S on and a cast on his foot. Ivan started to talk first about him being in a minor accident and getting a bad sprain. Leah said it looks worse than it is. It's just a bad sprained ankle. The hospital only kept him overnight for observation and he had just gotten home a half hour before she and James pulled up in the driveway. Brenna was so relieved and wanted to know why no one called her. Kim says right away, I wanted to call you because I know how close you are to dad, but everyone else said no that you would be home in a day and not to worry you because you and James had to get into a car and drive. They did not want them getting into an accident trying to get here. Brenna said I know that you didn't want me to worry but this is my dad too and I need to know what's going on with family too. Brenna gives her dad a big hug and asked him what happened and he explained that a teenager had stolen a car and was trying to outrun the police and side swiped his car. He reiterated to Brenna that he is fine and for her not to worry about him. He said he will be a little sore but thank God He kept him. She looked at James and goes over to him with tears in her eyes and he holds her and comforts her and let her know that God has everything in control and for her not to worry. One thing James tells Brenna is that her dad is in good shape and will be ok. He also asks Mrs. Smaller if she had any wine and she gets it for him to give Brenna a glass so she can calm down some. He is going to stay with Brenna a while because she is too upset for him to leave her like this. He knows that family is with her but soon she will be his family as well. He loves this girl and everything about her and all he wants to do is shield and protect her. The house is so cheery with everyone home and the Christmas tree is lit and the light are blinking and it just says all is well on the home front. After she has calmed down some James takes her by the hand and they walk out to the car and unload her clothes from the car and get the Christmas gifts that's in the large bags to store under the Christmas tree. After they put all the gifts under the tree James tells Brenna he needs to head home and his parents can see that he is home from her house. He calls home and his grandmother answers and says she knows why he has not got there and It's ok because she knows that Brenna is upset over her dad's accident. She tells him to take his time and they are going to drop by there to check on her dad themselves. They had heard that he was slightly injured in the accident and has been praying that all was well. They walk back into the house together and James announce that his family is coming over shortly. Mr. Smaller is overjoyed that his friend is coming over to the house to see him because they stay so busy now with the renovation on the studio that they don't get a chance to visit each other anymore. The studio will be complete in March. They completed the work outside of the building first so they can work on the inside when the weather gets to cold. They cannot wait to show off the building to the kids when they graduate. They are going to love it. James tell his grandparents that Johnny is already here as well and he is dropping off Camille to her parent's home. Terrence is going to Florida to see his wife and son and his parent's. They will be spending Christmas in Florida. Julie is spending Christmas day in Syracuse with Kevin and coming home after New Year's. James is flying to Washington, DC after Christmas with Brenna and her family to visit her mom's family. Now that the kids are getting married and will be on their own soon, Brenna's parents are thinking about moving to Charlotte, NC to be close to her dad's brothers and sisters. Well they have ten (10) more days before Christmas and Brenna is trying to think of something, they can do for the Christmas Holidays. She calls her friend Franklin and Arianna and they are traveling out of town to Connecticut to visit her grandparent for the holidays. They will be back in Atlanta for New Years. Brenna tell them that she has called her friend and they can meet up with their friend Brett and go out to dinner and then to a nice Jazz club. This would be very nice for them to do. She will call Brett and see what their plans are. In the mean time they will complete their shopping and cooking so everyone can relax at home with mom and dad. It's only a small amount of shopping that they have to do because they shopped the day after Thanksgiving and everything is basically done. After the Washington, DC trip they will fly to Charlotte NC and spend a few days there with her dad's sisters and brothers and then home for New Years to spend with James and his family. So not a lot of singing for the holidays because they will be booked solid pretty soon and can't get to visit family.

The concert is Sunday December 20th, at 6:00 PM. It is five days before the Christmas Holidays and Brenna and her family has an hour to get to the church. She spoke to Pastor Derrick and she will be there to help direct two of the songs for the choir that she taught them and maybe sing something if Pastor Derrick ask her too. Shekinah Praise just need some rest and relaxation and they won't be performing at all this Christmas. The choir did an outstanding job on their songs and after they finished the concert, Pastor Derrick asked Brenna and James to sing his favorite Christmas song and they did and they got a standing ovation. They sang to the Glory of God and they brought the house down. Brenna explains that they will be booked solid from the end of May thru the following year and if and when Pastor Derrick need Shekinah Praise, they will always schedule him in without cost because they grew up in his church and will be forever grateful to him for his help in showcasing their talent. Very good evening for them, even the Choir did an outstanding job on all their songs. Brenna promised Pastor Derrick one free concert a year. Well the concert is over and Brenna, James, Franklin and Arianna go to their favorite restaurant, Caesars Palace & Supper Club. Johnny and Camille came with them to the restaurant. They had a great time and then they all went home. Brenna went straight to bed. Tomorrow is another day for her and her mom and two sisters will put together their menu for Christmas day Friday. The four of them go to the market and pick up what is needed and return home and start to put it all together. They are only making enough dinner for Christmas day because they will be flying to Washington, DC to visit her mom's family and then to Charlotte, NC to visit her dad's sisters and brothers. They have a weeks' vacation to visit all and be back in Atlanta for the New Year. The family always make time to visit their family every two years. The family will stay three days in Washington, DC and three days in Charlotte, NC. Brenna let them know that they will all be invited to her wedding in July. She brought her fiancé' James with her to meet her family in both Washington, DC and Charlotte, NC. The family had a great time on vacation and now they are on their way back to the great city of Atlanta for the New Year's. They had planned a New year's dinner at Brenna's home and all of their friends were invited. The food was catered because they did not have the time to prepare before they left. The catering company assured them that it would be ready when they returned on New Year's Eve. Before the Smallers left the airport, they called the catering company and they were at the home now and everything had been set up for them. Pastor Derrick came over and let the caterers in and stayed until they returned from Charlotte. They were back in Atlanta at 4:00 PM. So, they had time to get home put everything away and go to church for the 10:00 PM service. Church was out promptly at 11:45 PM and they prayed until 12:00 AM bringing in the New Year. All friends and family were invited back to the Smaller's for early morning brunch. Everything really came together so nicely without them having to worry about if they had everything done completely.

Brenna's mom told them that she did not want to have to worry so she gave it to the caterers to have fun with. Pastor Derrick came and brought his whole family and they had a room set up down stairs for the kids and plenty of supervision to manage them. Everyone stayed until 8:00 AM the following morning and then they all went home except the Smaller family and siblings. New Year's Day everyone got up and prayed together and thanked the Lord for his financial Blessings that he had given to their families, and then they sat around and watched football and basketball the rest of the day and had brunch again and then dinner and later dessert.

Just before the kids went off to college, almost four years ago Brenna's dad, Julie's dad and James and Johnny's grandparents won the lottery and they had to keep it very quiet. It really was a substantial amount of money and the three families would never have to work again. They had won $765 Million. So, money was no problem for any of them for the rest of their lives. If they all watch how they are spending money they should all be fine and invest wisely. They brought the three families together and explained it and reminded them that they had to be very careful not to mention this to any one for their safety. The men in the homes continued to work and no one ever suspected that they had won this caliber of money. Everything was divided equally, and never was there an incident between the three families. So, for the business between them has been going great for the last four years. Their attorneys handled it so there wouldn't be any animosity between them. They have invested very wisely and have great financial People and attorney's that is handling all of the transactions and watching out for them. They are all business minded people and they are always involved with what is going on with their finances. Well the holidays are over and now everyone is packing and getting ready to travel back to Nashville for their final semester before graduation.

CHAPTER
SIX

The Beginning of Shekinah Praise Professional Career

Shekinah Praise have arrived back at their dorms and unpacked their clothing and getting ready for their classes. Shekinah Praise know that they have an upcoming event for January 15th. Brenna only booked a few concerts during the months of January and February because she, Arianna and Franklin have a play they are working on for the spring which is a part of their grade in Musical Theatre. So, their lives will be all work and no socialization of any kind if they want to get good grades and succeed in Musical Performing and Theatre.

Brenna is thinking that all members may not be present for this one concert, because everyone will be just returning to their dorms after the Christmas Holidays. Alice will be back in Florida and Terrence will be back in Atlanta. Brenna and Julie got the call that all members will be available for the January 15th concert. All members had a positive response. Terrence and Alice will be flying in. Brenna made sure all tickets had been purchased for Shekinah Praise trip and they are looking forward to seeing them.

Brenna, Franklin and Arianna will be doing their last play with Vander University. So, they will be quite busy for the next four months. This will also include adding their final touches to their CD. They have already acquired their picture for the CD cover. This will be their first picture of Shekinah Praise as a group. Brenna and Julie picked the one photo that was a wow factor for the entire group. It is one of their best photos. The photo just has to be sent to production to get printed up and packaged for the Market. They have really been working so hard to get their product into sales and praying that it does well. January 15th is in a few days and the Event is Saturday evening at 6:00 PM. They rehearsed on Friday evening and pulled all their songs together what they will be performing. Julie and Brenna think that Alice and Terrence should do the new song that he has written for his wife. Brenna has several songs that she has written herself. What makes this group so unique is every one writes their own material for the group and then they present it at their rehearsals and put their songs together. Each member can truly write great lyrics for songs and they use all their songs for Shekinah Praise and rewrite the one for other groups that they don't have a feel for the lyrics. Terrence himself is a great writer of songs and Alice does well and Brenna & Julie are so excited that they are on their team. Kevin will be performing with them for the next two concerts with Shekinah Praise. He is also developing his own brand for his Solo career with Brenna's sister Leah and brother, Ivan, as well as Julie's sister Dawn and her brother Brian. Kevin has met with all of the members, prior to him adding them as background singers and was pleased with how powerful they are at performing. They will be performing with him right away. There was no problem with them picking up his style of performing immediately. Kim, and Brenna's sister will be joining Shekinah Praise in April. Kim did the photo shoot with Shekinah Praise so when they start their scheduled events, she will be on the CD cover as one of the original members of Shekinah Praise. Brenna knows that Kim can really sing so she picked Kim to be with Shekinah Praise members as this will help their career as well. Everything seems to be falling into place and Brenna always remembers what her mom says about keeping God first in your life and see how he moves and makes things happen for you. Praise God she keeps him first.

Now what she needs to see is her boo James. She is so in love with this man. He is in her heart twenty-four seven. She will put up their wedding website in April. Julie is putting hers up the end of March. Their rehearsal went very well and they will be at the hall at 2:00 P.M. Saturday for sound check and music must be 100% ready for the performance. This is their first concert this year before their first CD hit the market and their music must be spectacular for this performance. The entire group is so excited about going professional. All they hear on the radio is about the upcoming new group that has risen up out of the Atlanta area and they can't wait until their CD hit the charts. So, this is putting pressure on Brenna and Julie to get this CD complete and on the market ASAP. Every place they go people are inquiring as to when their CD is coming out because they want to buy it. Shekinah Praise already have a great fan base on Twitter, Spotify and Face book.

James came to pick her up from the dorm to go to dinner. The two of them arrive at the restaurant and was seated and served. They couldn't get through their lunch for signing autographs. Finally, the owner of the restaurant came over and wanted to know who they were and some of the customers in the restaurant was explaining who they were. The owner Asked them to come in again and just sing something for the restaurant. Brenna is considering doing it because this will also help their career in the future. Brenna explains that they can do it once for them and then they will have to be booked like everyone else. The manager is thrilled and then tells Brenna they are thinking of bringing in a band to play soft music while their clients have dinner to see if this will bring in more clientele for the restaurant. The manager walks away thinking that this could be a great asset for the restaurant and have new bands their every weekend would certainly bring in more business for them. Brenna is also thinking as well because she is wondering if she can put together a band just to perform for restaurants on the weekends. Great idea to take back to the group. Although this would be handled by the family of the group because they don't want to be too stressed out with their performance and traveling to worry about the other part of the business. Brenna asked the manager if he had a piano and a MIC and he said yes and he showed them where it was and James walked over and began to play and Brenna began to sing and my goodness the place filled up inside of twenty minutes. Nothing was planned and it was a great evening for them. The Manager called them aside and gave them a sizeable donation and they weren't expecting anything. Brenna did not want to take anything for this and the manager told them he saw the good works in them and would love to help them on their way. They did several gospel and R & B songs that evening and the manager wanted to know if they could come back. Brenna told him they were all booked up right now and to call their office and they will see what kind of schedule they have within the upcoming months. This could work because they don't know when the tour will start exactly and this can be extra income for them. The Manager told Brenna that he would advertise this event as soon as they give him a date. They left the restaurant and on the way home Brenna called Julie to let her know what just occurred and they had fun laughing and praising God for the good things that he is doing in their lives, just wonderful things. Brenna told Julie that they would have to find a date to put the restaurant in because this would certainly help get them on the market much quicker. The week after the play is certainly a great weekend to do it and then they will be ready to take their finals and then they can sing at the restaurant until they are ready to tour. They called a meeting and talked it over with Shekinah Praise and everyone agreed that this would be a great event for them before they began their tour. Johnny's sisters have been given their positions as Fashionistas, stylist and makeup artist to travel with them and pick out their fashions for performing. Both of Johnny's sisters are in school for fashions and stylist and makeup artist. Their family is covering these positions because the group wants to keep it all in the family. They only have to find hair stylists for the men and women. Once they get the fashionista's and hair stylist on board, they will be ready to travel.

Now it's the day of the event for MLK, and sound check has been done and Shekinah Praise is ready to take the stage. They start off on a real high praise and then they slow down a little only to rise again to a very high level of praise. Nearing halftime of the concert, Shekinah Praise has everyone on their feet and they are at a spiritual high praise. Then they came off stage for intermission. Now it's time for them to reenter the stage for the second phase of the concert and Shekinah Praise is still on a spiritual high. Shekinah Praise takes it to another level and what a concert it was. The group did not have very many CD's at this time but all 375 CD's had been sold. Their tees, pens, hats and towels were gone within forty-five minutes after the concert. Everything sold that had their names on it and that had been displayed. The Theater asked them to please keep this date open for them for Black History month every year that they can. Brenna know that this will be one of their free concerts given back to the community. The manager as promised from the restaurant came out to the concert and walked over and shook Brenna's and James hand and he was introduced to the entire group and spoke briefly of what he would like them to do at the restaurant and they told him that after their play they would give him a firm date and he could advertise this event for them.

They left the Theatre on a high note and back to their dorms & apartments. The group was too tired to go out to eat. The only thing they were ready to do was hit their beds. The very next day they rested and got ready for their class work the next day. They had another performance coming up for Black history month in February. Shekinah Praise will be brushing up on some of their Negro Spirituals to present to the community. They keep some of these songs in their repertoire for special occasions like Black History month and MLK day as well as other occasions. Julie and Brenna called a rehearsal for the next two weekends to pull together their concert for February 19th for Black History month.

The days are flying by and its four days away from the Black history month concert for the Theater. Brenna, Franklin and Arianna are in full force with the end of semester play this week end from 7:45 PM to 10:45 PM for rehearsals for the concert for Black history month program here in Nashville. They can stop earlier if all their songs are completed. Brenna and Julie will not book any more events after the one for the restaurant until after their graduation then the fun and work begins. The Restaurant event will be fine because they don't have to constantly perform, they can play soft music when they are not singing. This should be a very easy task but they won't know until they do the performance.

It is day of the concert and Shekinah Praise is moving and getting everything in place for the concert in a few hours. Sound check is done and all songs has been rehearsed and they are ready to perform. Their concert started at 6 :00 PM and ended at 9:30 PM and it was one of their best performances that they had done in a while. All their songs were done to perfection and not one flaw in any of the songs. They did not hold a late-night concert because of the school kids even though it was the weekend they didn't want the kids staying up too late. This concert kind of told the story of the history of African Americans in the late 1800's leading up to the 20th century. They got so many compliments on this concert and they could not confirm for the next year because they will be touring as a New Artists and they are not sure which way their traveling adventures will take them but they will keep the theatre in mind for next year. As new Artist you just don't know that far in advance how things will work out.

At the Black History concert, they sold all their items, CD's, caps, tees, pictures and pens. This was not a ticket event, so their sales were from their own printing and productions and they really did well on their sales. They had a great Public Relations team. They had nothing left to return with them to their printing shop. With their last two concerts they had accumulated a great amount revenue from the sale of their items. Their parents are running the Shekinah Praise printing shop for them. They have two shops running now, one in the Nashville area and one in the Atlanta area. They are so blessed to have parents working with all of them to make this gospel group what it is today with God's help and it is thriving. James, Johnny, Kevin and Franklin run the business in Nashville when they are not so busy. Shekinah Praise goes home after the Black History concert very happy an exhausted but elated to know that their group is off to a great start. In seven days, they will perform at Carmichael's Restaurant for two nights as promised. The manager promised to let them sell their CD's and their products there at the restaurant which will be a big help to them. They are being promoted big time in Nashville for this Event. People all over the area are telling everyone to come out to this event. The manager has asked them to do two shows, one while they are having dinner and another one at 9:00 PM for show only. They will be performing R &B as well as gospel and then some requests if need be. Carmichael's is set up more less like a supper club and everyone must be dressed to get in. Very classy and upscale restaurant. They heard Kevin sing and heard the announcement that he would be moving on as a solo Artist and the manager wants him to perform there when he is not so busy performing and traveling. He has not agreed to do this yet because his parents want him to sing gospel only. Brenna thinks it would be a good idea for Kevin but he just doesn't want to do it because he is tired and want to rest up before the tour. His parents would prefer him doing gospel. Shekinah Praise prefer gospel as well but when it comes to making a living until, they are on tour and well established they will do some gospel Jazz. Brenna, Julie, James and Johnny want to only sing gospel but when they are in the restaurant, they will do some R & B.

The very next day Nashville performing Arts theatre called them to see if they will book a show for them the beginning of June and Brenna told Julie that maybe but they will consider it but they are both getting married in July so they have to have some time to get fitted with their gowns that have been ordered and all of their bride maids as well. If they get it booked and do it the very beginning of June, they can still do the concert. But this is the last booking until after they are married and ready to go on tour. The great part about this they ordered their dresses some time ago and they didn't wait until the last minute. They both rented the same hotel downtown Atlanta to have their reception. For this they got a discount on the hall. The hotel managers know the girls from their performances in the Atlanta area. Their parents took care of this for them and made sure that they did not book anything during these dates as they will be on their honeymoon. James knocked on her door as the was communicating with the staff in the hotel. She let James in and continued to talk to them. She asked if she could call them back within thirty minutes as she had to discuss it with the group to see if anyone had made any future plans on the first of June. All Brenna needed was to be in James arms and a kiss and hug from her future husband James and talk to him for a bit. Brenna explained the call from the hotel and he asked Brenna if they could get this concert in before the wedding and she told him yes but this would be the last one until she and Julie both got married and back from their honeymoon. All James said was YES. Julie was happy about this concert as well and they booked it and said this is it until after they got married. Julie called Kevin to see if he could be booked with Shekinah Praise as a solo artist and he said that was great. Brenna is also Kevin's Manager until he tells her otherwise. Kevin wants to sing a few of his songs with Shekinah Praise as a farewell to the group and hello to the new artist that he is becoming. It's a way of introducing Kevin during his last performance with Shekinah Praise. This will keep the couple together while they are on tour and traveling to other places. If Shekinah Praise is not booked, Julie can travel with her to help manage Kevin, her own husband. Julie has been asking Julie to step in and Manage Kevin but Julie doesn't want to do it because she wants to get pregnant right away and so does Brenna, but she has that covered for them. Terrance can manage them when they are on maternity leave. Brenna has been grooming him to do so. Brenna is very smart when it comes to managing and taking care of responsibilities. When Brenna mention this to Kevin, he had a problem with it until Terrence is fully trained and as of now, he wants Brenna to continue managing him. He likes the way she handles the group because she puts God First and is very easy to talk to and just has a way of handling people without a problem. She has a way of calming things down.

Brenna called the hotel back and told them they will be in on Friday evening to get the contract signed for this concert. She called the lawyers to make sure they are on the same page with them. The papers will be sent to Kevin's Lawyers in Syracuse, NY and their Lawyer in Atlanta. This will give them a week to get the lawyers here to Nashville to look over the contract and get it signed and ready for them to start preparing for this event. The lawyers will then fly to Nashville to discuss the contract with Shekinah Praise and Kevin Snow the Artist. This is great for Shekinah Praise as their CD will be Launched the end of May. Their tour is set for August and they are set to travel to twenty different states. Brenna has called a meeting for Shekinah Praise and Kevin Snow the Artist. In their meeting they discussed the next event in two weeks with Carmichael's Restaurant. They were so looking forward to doing this event for the restaurant.

It is the day of the event at Carmichael's restaurant and the first phase of the concert starts at 12:30 PM brunch time until 4:00 PM, and the next phase will be at be at 6:30 PM until 9:30 PM. The first phase went perfectly with Shekinah Praise singing softly gospel music and then some R & B mixed with Jazz that set the tone for a beautiful evening with your husband, wife or Finances' or significant other or just whomever you are with. The second phase of the program was as beautiful as the first phase. Just a great evening for Shekinah Praise and the restaurant as well. The manager was very pleased with the evening and told them he wished he could have them the remainder of the year. The dinner guest was equally please with their dinner and their entertainment during dinner hours. On Saturday, the second day at Carmichael's Restaurant was a repeat of Friday evening. The picture-perfect dinner setting with great music and great dinner guest was just excellent. The first phase of Saturday evening was absolutely beautiful and the second phase was on a higher level than the first. They wanted to leave a great impression of their talent at the restaurant. All around a great evening for Shekinah Praise. They performed some classical, R & B and gospel jazz Brenna and James sang the Song God has Smiled on Me and it was just so beautiful to see the two of them sing and just look at each other with such love and affection for each other. They announced to the Restaurant that they were getting married in July and so was two other couples in their group. As they closed down the first phase for intermission, soft music continued to play throughout the intermission. As they reentered Carmichael's restaurant again to continue the second phase of the evening, it was a repeat of the first phase, absolutely beautiful. They finished the night with Kevin and Julie singing their love song to each other. The Manager was completely blown away with their performance. All he could do was shake his head and smile and wish that he could keep this group of singers at his restaurant because he knew what it would do for his business. The Manager wanted to know if they had any other days free to work for him. Brenna told him that they have to be back in school to finish up their finals. Well they finished up the night and everyone left the restaurant for the evening. They are all going to church on Sunday morning. Brenna always feel that if they can perform the night before Sunday, it will be a blessing to make it to church and sing for the Lord.

Brenna is up early Sunday morning but not feeling well so she goes to church anyway and comes straight back to the dorm right after service and drink some hot lemon ginger tea and go straight to bed. They will be practicing for their play tomorrow. Once they get this play out of the way they can concentrate on their class work and finals. Brenna, Franklin and Arianna are just exhausted because of the play and then the performance done for Black History and the performance they just completed at Carmichael's restaurant. Now they are on to the completion of the play and it will be presented next week, then they can relax and finish up their finals and be on course for graduation. Their friends will be supporting them next week when they present the play. The week went smoothly with their rehearsals of the play and the studio is all set up for the performance and they have performed the play all week with everything in place and the first two rehearsals they got all the glitches out of the way and now it is flowing together. They had a mock sit in for the play to get feedback from the student body and some of the faculty and all said it was a great performance each evening they sat in. There were a few remarks showing them where it needed to be fixed and they implemented it in the right places. After the third run through the director said this is a rap and it is great. He gave them two thumbs up. All the performers were extremely happy. They will run through it one time for the next few evenings and it would be fine for the performance. After Brenna got in her dorm, she called James just to talk and let him know how much she really loved him and to see what time he was coming own Thursday evening for their first performance. It started at 2:30 PM and ends at 5:45. They made small talk about their upcoming nuptials the invitations that they had to complete and send out. James asked Brenna if she misses him and she says of course I miss you but pretty soon we will be together and won't have to call each other because we will be by each other's side. James smiles and tells her that I can get used to. We also have to check in with our parents about the graduation party at my house. All the parents are planning a party for their kids at the Newly Renovated Studio but they don't know it. They are bringing in a few local artists to perform for them. James and Brenna finished up their conversation and they went off to bed.

Thursday evening came and they were ready for the play. Brenna was the first one to start off the song and then the acting part joined in by Franklin and then Arianna. As the other cast enter in and did their part in the play it became a great musical play. They had their intermission and then on with the second part of the play. The play was absolutely fantastic and when the first show ended everybody was on their feet. The first show was a sellout. It was not an empty seat in the theatre. James waited out front with Julie, Kevin, Johnny, Camille and some of their other friends. They went to the café just around the corner from the theatre to grab a bite to eat before the next show. The next show started at 6:45 PM and ended at 9:25 PM The second show was as great as the first show. The first show they just had to get through it and the second show was much more fun to do. It just felt right knowing all the pieces fell right into place after the second go round. The next three evenings were as great. Brenna's, Franklin and Arianna's parents were there every night to support them. What an awesome time they had with this play. Each evening the cast really showed off their talent. Their director was so happy and pleased with how the play was presented. Now for the next month and a half they will concentrate on their class work and grades. This is very important for Brenna and the entire Shekinah Praise group. They want to get busy with graduation and then home to begin their work on their tour. They have the one concert left to do the first of June and then they can stay in Atlanta until their wedding. No more concerts after this on because the girls ae getting married in July. Julie and Brenna are so excited about this. They will have some time to spend with their husbands before they go on tour and then they will be touring together in different states so this will make for an extended honeymoon for the two couples.

The entire Shekinah Praise group finished up their testing and now they are waiting for graduation on May 13th. Brenna went down to where their grades were being posted and she saw her name there. She would be graduating Summa Cum Laude. She almost passed out when she saw her grades, but she knew that she had put everything she had in studying for her test and it paid off big time. Instead of them partying they were out doing concerts and learning new songs for the group and the church, so they did not have time to mess up their grades. They were just a great group of kids that knew and loved the Lord and did what was right. They were graduating on Friday morning and leaving for Atlanta on Saturday morning. Their graduation was pretty lengthy and they sat through it and got their diplomas and then they took pictures with their friends and family and then they were ready to leave. They had packed their cars right after the graduation ceremony to be ready to leave on Saturday morning. Their parents had invited their friends over on Sunday evening for their graduation party. They gave the kids their gift on Sunday morning. A set of keys and told them they wanted to take them to a nice place on Sunday for their graduation and they could have their graduation party when they wanted to at home. So the kids were so confused about the keys but they went along with it because they did not know what they were getting. Brenna and Julie's parents told them to take the keys with them on Sunday. Brenna thought that she was getting her own home and so did Julie and the rest of the kids of the parents that had won the lottery. Julie and Brenna had the keys but did not know what to do with them.

Everything was planned down to people being invited as guest to perform for them. They all got dressed up like they are really going to a ball room and the place is set up like a ball room with lots of people all around and then Brenna saw an Artist from Syracuse, NY and some from Atlanta and they just burst out crying and the entire Shekinah Group was there dressed all in white as they were and it was too funny when she saw them all.. Their parents stood up and had several Artists to perform for them and then her parents along with Kevin and his parents introduced the entire group to come up and their parents told Brenna and Julie that the keys were for their Studio and this was their gift to them for recording. The girls could not stop crying but as the parents told them that they would discuss details later. After the two groups had performed, they had a couple of their friends, R & B artist to perform for the party. Then Kevin Snow introduced the new artist of Atlanta as "SHEKINAH PRAISE" and asked them to come up and perform for their friends and they gave the performance of their lives. Shekinah Praise performed better than they had ever performed before. Kevin's dad wanted to book them at his church when they are off tour and they will have a ticket event at his Church in Syracuse for them. Everybody was on their feet when they finished performing. They had the Atlanta Herald and other news reporters there to capture the new group. This was one of the greatest things their parents had ever done for them. Now that all the graduations parties are over and they all were great, but nothing measured up to what their parents did for them and they really loved it all. Brenna and Julie are on cloud nine and can't get over what their parents did for them. So now they have their own studio to come in and manage it the way they had planned. No more calling studios in the area to rent time for recordings. They can record whenever they want to and even rent when they want to if they are not using the studio.

Their phone started ringing and didn't stop until they all went to bed. This was the grandest evening that any of them had ever had. Brenna started getting calls early as 9:00 AM the very next morning but had to explain to everyone that they are going on tour in August. Then they wanted to know what will they be doing until August but Brenna was very happy to inform them that she and James would be getting married in July and also Julie too. So, they had to take some time to put together another concert in Nashville that had been booked for June 1st. This is their last concert until they go on tour to present their new CD.

James calls Brenna to let her know that he is on his way over and when he arrives, they call Julie, Kevin, Franklin, Arianna and the rest of group to meet them at the studio to see how it works. Kevin knows how to operate the equipment and so does Terrence. Brenna and Julie know how to operate most of it but the latest equipment, they will have to take some classes from an engineer to learn how to operate it. They will call up some of the engineers in the area of see if they can teach them how to operate the equipment. Then a light bulb went off in their head, Johnny and Terrence has engineering degrees in music which will go a long way for them and they can teach Brenna and Julie how to operate the new equipment. Problem solved.

Shekinah Praise are in the studio everyday rehearsing for the June 1st concert. The concert is this weekend, and they have to travel back to Nashville for this concert. They rented a tour bus for their travels because they don't want to be so tired when they get there from driving themselves. The bus is leaving Thursday evening at 1:00 PM. They are staying at the hotel in Nashville on Thursday and Friday and leaving early Saturday morning for Atlanta. Shekinah Praise arrived in Nashville and checked into their hotel and the group was up early Friday morning ready for sound check and rehearsal for the concert tonight. The music seems to be on point and their rehearsal were great. They will be ready for 6:00 PM this evening. The bus took them back to the hotel for a little relaxation before they have to travel back over to the theater and get dressed for the concert. They get back to the theatre and to their dressing room and was told by the concert host that they would come and get them when they are ready for them to go on stage. They noticed that the theatre is completely packed. Now Shekinah Praise is making their way to the stage and everyone is on their feet clapping and shouting out their name. Shekinah Praise, Shekinah Praise, Shekinah Praise. As Brenna hits the stage and lets Shekinah Praise know that when she calls their name, come and take their position. Brenna steps on the stage as the host introduces her as the manager and one of the lead singers of Shekinah Praise, she prepares them for their entry and they join her on stage. She does not waste time in Starting the concert they begin to sing. The first song was led by Kim, Brenna's sister. She stepped out and opened up her mouth and what a melodious voice she has. She really did a great job on the song and not even a waver in her voice. She was perfect and everyone was on their feet when she finished. Terrence and Alice sang their new duet and then of course the Bride and Groom James and Brenna took it to another level. Everyone in the group did a song and each time they would take it to different heights in the program. Anyone of Shekinah Praise members can take a song and sing They are the most gifted and newest groups around Atlanta and everyone is on fire to hear them. They are on a complete spiritual high as they finish up the first half of the concert. They go to intermission and family members are selling CD's, Tee shirts, photos of the group, pens and hats. They sold out of everything that they had. As they make their way back to the stage, they took it to another level of singing and as they finished up their concert, Shekinah Praise was on such a high that it took them some time to get settled down. They got plenty of praise and standing ovations. Kevin was making his announcement about his leaving Shekinah Praise and going out on his own as a Sole artist. This was his last appearance as a member of Shekinah Praise. Kevin let them know that he will continue touring with them most of the time but the Lord has moved him out and along as a Soloist. He explains that his wife is a member of Shekinah Praise and he will always be somewhere near them but not all of the time. He started his Solo career last year but kept Shekinah Praise as his backup singers and now they are moving on and he has acquired their family members as his backup singers now and he is still in business with his band.

Shekinah Praise have put together their new band and it is fantastic. They had to hire all new people and since all of the group is in music, they did not have any problem in acquiring what they needed. Kevin introduced his background singers and his band. He had them to come on stage as well. As they came up Shekinah Praise came down off the stage so his group could perform a number for this concert. They were all great and the new singers seemed like they had always been together with Kevin Snow. Kevin Snow then introduced his manager as Brenna Smaller and everyone was so excited that she was still managing his career as well as Shekinah Praise's manager. Kevin explained that Brenna was so talented at what she does and he did not want to lose her as his manager because he doesn't know anyone that can multitask the way she does. His future wife is her assistant but he doesn't want that to be a conflict of interest because they want to have children right away and the both of them plan to raise their children together which we have already agreed to. They have been best friends since they were eleven years old so James and I cannot separate them so we just say yes to whatever they want and keep them happy. But all jokes aside we are all a very close group that met in college and I have been with them for the last four years. I will bring back to stage my manager as she does have some news that she would like to share with you about Shekinah Praise. When Julie gets back on stage, she asked, did everyone enjoy themselves. Well the good news is that our new CD will be coming out on June 20th an everyone should go and purchase one. We will also begin our tour in August to support our new CD. So please watch out to see when we will be in the Nashville or Atlanta Area or you can check our website to see what city we will be in.

The concert ended at 10:00 PM. The bus took them back to their hotel where they had a room set up at the hotel for them to have a little celebration and food. It was a very nice evening for them and they turned in. Saturday morning they're up early and on their way back to Atlanta. They arrived back in Atlanta Safe.

CHAPTER
SEVEN

The Wedding's for Brenna and Julie

Brenna and Julie are so excited about their upcoming nuptials. They are both rushing around making sure all their plans are being carried out. The flowers have been preordered but they have to go and visit the florist with their parents to get the pieces for the church and to make sure the center pieces for the reception at the hotel are the correct pieces that they ordered for their wedding on Thursday and Friday. Julie is getting married on Thursday and Friday Brenna is getting married and they are each other's best friend and maid of honor. The four of them are flying out together on Sunday morning at six AM to Jamaica (Sandals Resorts) and a week later to (DR)Dominican, Republic for a week for their honeymoon. James and Kevin planned their honeymoon trip for the girls because they felt that they are well deserving of it. They talked it over with the girls and they loved the idea that they were going to be at the same places at the same time. What a blessing the girls thought to themselves that they would be near each other on their honeymoon. This makes Brenna and Julie's day. None of them will be spending every waking moment with each other but they planned to be back in Atlanta around the same time so they can start preparing for their upcoming tour in August.

Reporters are following them around and asking them questions about their wedding and they really don't want to talk about it but

Brenna and Julie decided to give them a little news so they can leave them alone to get all their plans over looked and ironed out before their wedding day. Brenna gave them the dates of their wedding. The reporter wanted to know if they would stay in the Atlanta area and the answer to them was yes for now but they don't know what the future may hold for them. Is Shekinah Praise planning on releasing their CD anytime in the future and they answered yes, the end of June. Does either one of you plan to have children in the near future and their answer was yes within a year. Will you have the babies/children to travel with you, or will you have nannies to care for them? The girl's response to the reporters was the babies will be traveling with us and a nanny as well. When the infants are older, they will be looked after by our parents especially when we are traveling. All new infants should be given an opportunity to spend as much time with their moms as possible so they can be nurtured and bond with moms when they are in their early stages of life. Will either one of you breast feed the babies? Of course, said Brenna when her little ones are first born, they certainly will be breast fed because it is much healthier for them. When we are home, we will take care of them ourselves Julie answered yes as well that she plans on breast feeding her babies. And because they will have touring buses and flights their infants will be with them during their nursing stages. Brenna tells them this is all the time that they have to talk to them today because they have appointments that they have to keep and thanks it is a pleasure talking to you.

Brenna has dragged James around and he's so loveable and not complaining at all. He knows in the end that he is getting a beautiful and loving young lady that he loves with all his heart. He looks at her like there is no other around him but her and she is his chocolate cake. He looks at her and just takes her in his arms and kisses her until she just says my, my young man we need to calm down and relax. He smiles and tell her 19 more days and you're all mine. She smiled and was in his arms again in seconds. She loves him so much and it's even harder for them to control themselves. She and Julie talk all the time about their wedding night and they're curious because they are both still virgins and they're kind of frightened somewhat at the same time about it. The girls will just have to trust their future husbands. Julie tells Brenna that Kevin is so gentle with her as well but he gets so excited and nervous when they are kissing and wants to cut the kiss short because he doesn't trust himself with her as they get closer to their wedding date. He tells Julie that he loves her and don't want to put her in a position where they can't wait for their wedding night. Brenna & Julie laugh because the guys are rushing home to take cold showers. The girls are very much aware of how hard it is to wait but they both had promised their moms that they would remain virgins until they got married. All Brenna and Julie talked about is how they are going to slip away for an hour after the marriage to be with their husbands. The four of them are at the venue that they rented for the wedding and Brenna and Julie walks away to see all of the hall and then they walk back only to hear James tell Kevin that it has gotten extremely hard to wait on Brenna before their wedding night but he loves and adore her so much that he will walk on water to make sure that she has a great wedding night. Kevin agrees totally. He tells James that he's happy its only eighteen more days. He says Julie changed his life completely, because at one point in his life when he was living in Syracuse and out of the arch of Jesus Christ he was getting out of control and his mom and dad had to talk to him and get him back on course. He came back into his father's church and got saved and started singing and he is totally committed to Jesus Christ. After he went off to college and met Julie, he was absolutely in love with her but she was hung up on Johnny and Johnny broke her heart. He knew that she was struggling with a situation with her current boyfriend and it ended and he was there to pick up the shattered pieces of her life and heart. He had been trying to talk to her but she wasn't responding. Then one day he walks over to her because she looked so sad that day and started a conversation with her and into the conversation asked her to go on a date with him and she accepted and the rest is history. He is now waiting for eighteen more days and she will be his wife. Kevin met her friend Brenna and they hit it off very well. They all became best of friends after he met Brenna's friend James and her college friends Franklin and Arianna. They realized that they were all into music and loved singing and they put together a group of singers that loved singing and praising the Lord. They became great singing buddies as well. There were a few conflicts with Julie and Johnny because they were an item back home in Atlanta but Johnny wanted to venture out with someone else other than home girl and he lost the love of his life Julie by doing that. Julie is a survival and all her troubles were ironed out pretty quickly after she met now the love of her life Kevin Snow. Franklin and Arianna are getting married In October, so there are more weddings coming up this year for the group. Johnny has already asked Camille for her hand in marriage and their wedding is in December. Terrence and Alice are already married and Brenna's sister Kim is already engaged to a young man she met in college Alvin Matthews. He is a great young man that seems to love Kim very much. They plan to get married before Brenna and Julie. So, this is some of the history of their group.

They have reached the florist and the first person they see is uncle Hayward Wilson, Brenna's uncle. He loves working at the flower shop and is willing to give Brenna and Julie a discount because he is their uncle and he made sure they came to him to give the shop the business. Uncle Hayward has retired and his sons are running the business now but he is up most days and in the Floris shop like he has not retired. Hayward still brings in a lot of business since he turned the Business over to his sons Everyone in the area knows him. Sometimes he acts like he hasn't retired and is still running things and they just let him have his way because they know he means well. Hello Uncle Hayward said Brenna and Julie. It's good to see you today and did you make sure we are going to have our flowers for our wedding. Uncle Hayward with the most courageous smile ever on his face responded yes you know that I am always going to make sure you have the prettiest flowers for both your weddings on Thursday and Friday. He loves his nieces very much and her best friend Julie who call him uncle as well. Uncle Hayward tells them they have the long skinny vases that they are requesting for all the guest tables. He walks them in and then tells the manager that his sons have heard that his two nieces are here with their parents to confirm their order of flowers for their wedding. They want to view the vases to make sure they are what they wanted for the tables. The girls love the long skinny vases that uncle Hayward has shown them. Oh, these are the ones both girls replied. The only difference in their flowers are their color scheme. Brenna has a few tables where the vases are not long and skinny and so does Julie and they are different in that respect. They both have a different taste on the smaller vases. Brenna's color scheme is Dahlia, White and Yellow and Julie's is Teal, Yellow and Red with trimmings of teal in their bouquet. Julie's bride's maid's dresses are teal and their bouquets are teal, yellow and red flowers. Brenna's girls' dresses are Dahlia, and their bouquets are, Dahlia, white and yellow with trimmings of gold and greenery. They have six girls each as bride's maids, and two flower girls and a ring bearer.

After they had taken care of all their business with the flowers, they wanted to take uncle Hayward out to lunch and he is more than happy to go with them as they are his family and he loves his family and loves to eat. He has a favorite restaurant and he didn't waste any time telling them where he wanted to go. Brenna sometimes hang out with her cousins Dereck, Jerry and Ryan, her uncle Hayward's sons. They are the athletes in the family. The three of them played basketball in high school and college. When they went off to college, they did not spend very much time together, but they do support them with their group Shekinah Praise. Jerry and Ryan never try to sing because that is not their God given talent. Dereck is a rapper and he wants to work with Brenna and Julie in the studio. He has an engineering degree to work in the musical field also, reporting broadcasting, television and radio broadcasting. He writes material for another artist so he is going to be a great asset to their studio and to the group as well. He has his own studio and most of his equipment was stolen from him. He was only left with several computers and an expensive keyboard. His most expensive equipment was taken out of his studio and he would have to basically start all over again because he did not have all the equipment insured. Dereck has a great mind and a great eye for talent, he will certainly bring in more business for the studio. Daily the girls are at the studio and this is their last week dealing with the studio until after their wedding. Dereck, Terrence, Johnny and some of the other cousins will be running the operations of the Studio until after the wedding.

This is a family business and family will run it and Brenna and Julie will make the majority of the decisions as usual and take advice from their parents and business minded cousins that are capable of adjusting and running the business until they return from their honeymoon. All managers will be checking constantly with their lawyers to make sure that operations are one hundred percent up to standard. They don't need any unnecessary glitches coming up when they are away, or in the future.

The days are racing by and it's nearing Julie's and Brenna's wedding. Brenna, Julie and their parents has taken care of all the flowers two weeks ago. It is now Tuesday, two days before Julie's wedding and the girls are on their way to the bridal shop for Brenna's last fitting and to pick up her gown. Brenna had lost more weight and the dress had to be altered again. It fitted her perfectly and Julie laughs and tells Brenna just don't lose any more weight by Friday. Julie has two more days and Brenna has three more days. They thought of a double wedding but Brenna did not want to share in Julie's day and Julie felt the same way. They both wanted their own separate wedding. Julie had already packed up her dress and all her undergarments that she needed. Brenna is picking up her dress and all her undergarments as well. They both ordered two other dresses for their reception but different which is appropriate for their reception. Both the dresses are white but are made different and they are absolutely gorgeous and a little shorter for the reception. They won't have to pin up their wedding gowns for dancing. These gowns have one strap across the shoulder, one with flowers and the other with lace and they are lighter in weight. Their parents did not spare any expenses on their dresses. Brenna and Julie used Shari's Bridal shop for their dresses and accessories. After Brenna had done her last fitting, she stopped at the lingerie shop for her undergarments that had been ordered for her and awaiting her pick up. Their shoes had been purchased and was waiting for them at home. Now that Brenna had picked up all her dresses for the wedding, she needed to see her fiancé' James. She had not seen him all day. Brenna and Julie called James and Kevin after they had gotten home to pick them up because they needed to do some paperwork at the studio for two hours. They were done in less than two hours. Brenna walked into the other office where James was working and he stopped and came over and took her into his arms and told her how much he loved her and gave her one of his earth shattering kisses that he likes planting on her. It shook her to the core. He really needed her right now and she knew it but he knows he had to stop. There are boundaries that he is not willing to cross until they are married. He thanks the Lord every day for giving him such a beautiful young lady to love and be his wife. But he has another three days before he is married to her. He loves her so much that he cannot focus clearly when she is around. They have both worked so hard to remain celibate until marriage. All they have to do now is get through the next three days. As they are walking out, they see Julie in Kevin's arms and she seems like she is crying and Brenna becomes upset because she doesn't want to see her friend upset nearing her wedding day. Julie stands back out of Kevin's arms and then she turns and sees Brenna and he comes rushing out to her and they cry together. Brenna asked Julie what was wrong and she tells Brenna that it is so hard to wait until marriage and Brenna tells Julie that she just had the same conversation with James and they just kissed and walked away together and then they saw her and Kevin being upset. I am just glad it's nothing but love and they both laugh. Julie knows that Kevin loves her very much and the waiting is unbearable sometime. So, Brenna tells her that its only two more days and everything will be perfect. They both laugh and say the waiting is getting to us. Julie tells Brenna I thought that I really loved Johnny and there could never be another one for me but I was so wrong about that. It took me meeting and falling in love with Kevin to understand what being in love really was. She says that she and Johnny was more infatuated with each other than anything else because as soon as he met another girl he was moving on and that showed her that he was really never in love with her. We were never like you and James. You two always knew what you wanted and you remained in love. The two of you had a solid foundation and Johnny and I did not. That is real love Brenna. You two never wavered in how you felt about each other. I know said Brenna, my mom always taught me that when you meet the right one you will know it and with James, I knew that I had met my partner for life. I prayed every night asking God to let him be the right guy for me and he was always so very sweet and fateful to me. He would never let anyone get between the two of us. There was one girl Tamika that really liked James but he took care of this situation from day one and that said a lot about his character and his fatefulness to me. Julie said to Brenna, I kind of knew that Johnny had roaming eyes after I came up to college where he was. He would always get a funny look in his eyes when I was near him and it always seemed like he was or wanted to be somewhere else. But I found out rather quickly that he was seeing someone else. When I met Kevin and he was so nice and sweet to me and when Johnny found out that I was dating Kevin then he wanted to play the victim as if he really cared about me but I just told him I was not up for his games and I had seen him with Camille. This is when Camille started to ask him about me and he did not want to talk about it. She even asked me what was I to him and I told her and she was not happy with him or I. Camille could not understand how he could lie to her knowing that he was with Julie. The last time Camille came to her about Johnny, Julie told Camille they were finished and she could move on with him. He said to Julie several times that he just wanted her back. I tried to get back together with him but nothing was the same and I just could not trust him anymore. Camille kept her eyes on Julie until she saw he out on a date with Kevin Snow. Johnny wanted Camille and me to and you know that was not going to work for me. After a year and a half with Kevin, we got engaged and things have been great between us since we met. I really and truly love him so much Brenna. I think he would have been the only one to really turn my world upside down. If we had broken up, Johnny is a sweet guy as well but he didn't know what he wanted when it came to me and Camille. I took charge of my own life and broke it off with him and Kevin became my main priority in life. He stayed with me until I worked out all the feelings I had for Johnny and then the two of us became very serious and that led to our getting engaged to be married. There is no one else for me Brenna but Kevin. Well two more days and I will be Mrs. Kevin Snow. So, I have waited this long Brenna, I think I can wait two more days. Julie and Brenna both laughed.

Pastor has checked in with both Julie and Brenna with their plans for their wedding and all the decorations for the church is in place to be delivered early Wednesday evening and Pastor lets them know not to forget the runner for the church. He tells them that this seems like the things that most brides forget before they walk down the aisle. They both have check lists and this has been checked off. The runners have been delivered to the church already and the flowers will be there on Wednesday evening for decorating the church. Brenna's and Julie's moms are on top of these things for the girls. They don't want the girls getting stressed out before the wedding. For the flowers there are cup holders in the church on all the pews and all they have to do is change the flowers in the cup holders for Julie's wedding on Thursday and then again on Friday for Brenna's wedding. Brenna and James are singing for Kevin and Julie's wedding and Kevin and Julie are singing for Brenna's wedding. The entire group Shekinah Praise has an active role in their wedding. So, they did not have to hire extra singers for anything. Shekinah Praise is doing it as an engagement gift to the two couples. Terrence is doing a narrative piece with his wife Alice. They are kind of like the chaperones for both weddings as well. Pastor has checked to make sure all music is appropriate for church and he knows that it is but he likes to check because he is the pastor and church etiquette means a lot to him. Everyone must abide by the laws of the church. The kids are like his friends as well as he's their pastor for they grew up in his church and he is only about eight (8) years older than they are. The senior Pastor has retired and he is now the pastor of their church. On Tuesday night as scheduled at the church, Julie and Brenna did their wedding rehearsal for the ceremony and Pastor was very pleased at them for remembering all of it without having to go through it a dozen times. On Wednesday evening they both had their rehearsal dinner at Shae Palmer' Restaurant together. The large dining hall was open for just the two families. The other two dining halls was for their regular customers. They are such a close nit family and friends' group that they could get together and celebrate this rehearsal dinner together. It was just Brenna's and Julie's immediate family only and their wedding party. Their Minister prayed for the rehearsal dinner. It was a great dinner for the two brides and their family.

It is the day of Julie's wedding and she is so nervous and needs to talk to her mom and her mom tells her not to be afraid that Kevin loves her and he will take care of her because she is a virgin. She calms down for a little while after talking to her mom and then her mom kisses her on the cheek and leaves, and she needs to talk to her best friend Brenna. Brenna comes into her bedroom and they talk about their wedding night and Julie is uptight about the whole thing all over again. Brenna tells her that it will be fine. Kevin will know how to handle your relationship very carefully because he has waited this long and he will be gentle with you because he loves you very much. Brenna is trying to calm her friend own and she thinks its working just fine. Brenna prays with Julie and then Julie prays with and thanks God for sending her such a nice young man to love and ask him to keep them in his care at all times no matter what the situation is and what they are going through. Brenna goes into the kitchen and gets a cup of Chamomile tea and get the Blackberry Brandy and put a shot of the Blackberry brandy in the tea with lemon and within five to seven minutes Julie has relaxed and she is ready to get into the limo and go to the church. She has totally relaxed and smiling and enjoying herself before she walks down the aisle. Shekinah Praise has rendered the music for the ceremony. All of her bride maids' dresses are a lighter shade of teal. Now every is in place, her mom has been escorted down into the sanctuary, now it's Brenna's time to walk in and she comes down the aisle looking stunning in the teal dress that she has on and next the flower girls in white with teal sashes dropping teal red and gold flower petals followed by the ring bearer in a white tuck with teal tie and teal handkerchief. Now the music changes an it's time for Julie and her dad to come in on the wedding march and Julie looks so beautiful in her wedding gown with her yellow, white. Teal and red roses bouquet. The church is decorated so beautifully and Julie, and her bridesmaids are stunning in their teal dresses and their beautiful bouquets and her husband to be and groomsmen are so very handsome as well. When Julie gets to the altar, her brother sings a song for her and she did not know where the sound was coming from until Brenna says softly that it's your brother in the choir stand. No one knew that her brother could sing that well. After they said their vows and the Pastor has pronounced them husband and wife, Julie looks at Brenna gives her the most beautiful smile and tells her that I did it. Brenna gives her a smile and a big hug after they got out in the vestibule area of the church. The tells Julie girl you got this and they hug again. When Brenna looks at Kevin, he is wiping his forehead and James is talking to him. It seems like they are both a little frighten of the wedding night. James looks at Brenna and holds up one finger indicating to her one more day and they will be married as well. The wedding was so beautiful and it was just a perfect day for Julie. They shook hands with all their guest and then they were on their way to take pictures. This took about an hour and thirty minutes. When they arrived at the hotel in downtown Atlanta, everyone having a blast. The four of them, Brenna, James, Julie and Kevin walked down the private entrance to the ballroom to see it before everyone entered. It was spectacular with all the flowers arranged so pretty and in places as requested and this said a lot for the manager in charge of the hotel and their wedding planners. Soon the doors will open to the ballroom for their quest as soon as they go backout the private entrance before the quest sees them. Brenna and Julie, Kevin and James are so excited about the ballroom and how everything looks. It's just picture, perfect said Julie and we really have to thank our parents for coming down and checking everything and making sure we don't have to worry about anything. All quest has taken their sets and waiting for the Bride and Groom to make their way in. As, Alice and Arianna announce the Bride and Groom, Mr. and Mrs. Kevin Snow, they came in so sweetly dancing with Mics in their hands singing to each other. This was perfect for the two of them. Alice takes her Mic and ask the Bride and Groom to make their way to the floor for their first dance as husband and wife. Then the Bride dances with her father and the Groom dances with his mother, just beautiful and then the bride maids and their groomsmen dance and the Bride and Groom take their seat at their table.

Such a beautiful wedding. Julie gets up with the Mic in her hand again and sings to Kevin. He was shocked because she did not tell him that she was going to do this at all. Brenna knew she was going to do it because they talked about how they were going to surprise them with a song. Kevin and Julie stayed on the floor for about three dances and then they disappeared for a period of time for Julie to change into her tea length dress so she can dance and enjoy herself without tripping up in her wedding gown. She asks Brenna to come up stairs to help her with her wedding dress. After she takes the wedding dress off, she is trembling again and Brenna tells her to just relax and enjoy her husband. Brenna leaves the room and Kevin comes in and he is as nervous as Julie but he manages to remove his coat and then they shared one of the most intimate moments together. It was just perfect and they had to rush to get Julie into her new gown for their reception.

Julie and Kevin quickly refreshed themselves and Julie changed into her dress. Julie had to make sure that she was ok to go down stairs. Their wedding night can't come soon enough especially with the teasing that she had just gotten with Kevin. She looked equally as stunning as she did in her wedding gown. Kevin pulled her into his arms again and told her how much he loved and adored and wanted her and she responded with I love you to sweetheart but we need to hurry and get out of this room before I change my mind about going back to our reception. Kevin looks at her and said I agree we must leave now.

Julie and Kevin returned to their reception and it was one of the best receptions that she has ever been to because it was all hers. Finally, she takes Kevin's hand and tells him that she has to talk to Brenna and she ask him if he wants to come with her and he tells her that he wants to talk to James for a few minutes about their honeymoon. She finds Brenna and she could hardly contain herself. I love this man more than life itself. We will talk when we both are married. I don't want to ruin it for you. I am so happy and loved that I don't know what to do with myself. Kevin tells James that he was so excited that he was a complete nervous wreck with his now wife. He tells James that they will talk about their nerves later on after he is married on tomorrow. Just try and keep it together man because I thought I was going to be just great but I was a bundle of nerves. They visited all of their guess table's together and said thanks for coming and hope they are having a great time. Their parents bought nice souvenirs for all the tables and great gifts for the bridesmaids and Shekinah Praise too.

Well one wedding down and one to go tomorrow. They all make their way to their hotel rooms to prepare for Brenna's wedding tomorrow evening. They are having an early morning brunch for Brenna's and James family at her home. The brunch will start at 8:00 AM and end at 10: AM. This will give Brenna time to go back to her room an relax before the wedding at 3:00 PM. Brenna's parents hired a staff of people to set up the Brunch and clean up afterward. Julie will help Brenna get dressed in her room before they go to the church. They will be taking pictures at 5:45 PM on the grounds of the hotel and reception will be 7:00 PM. The hotel grounds are stunning and the pictures will be perfect with all the shrubbery and lightening that surrounds the hotel. It's just picture perfect for their photo shoot. Brenna's mom comes to her room and wants to know if she wants to talk and she is glad that she did because she does want to talk to her mom about her wedding night and maybe her mom can keep her calm for tomorrow because she is a nervous wreck right now. She looks at her mom and her mom can see the tears in her eyes and she comes and sits on the side of the bed with her and tells her it's going to be alright and don't be afraid of her wedding night. She tells Brenna that James loves her very much and he will not hurt her at all. Young lady you just have to trust your husband, and everything will be fine. Brenna is so naïve and she sees it in her eyes. Then she asks the question will it hurt her and her mom tells her only for a second and it will go away very quickly. She wants to know if she can stay in the room with her tonight and she ask her what her husband was going to do without her. She smiles and say she will send Leah to stay in the room with her. Leah and Brenna talked for a while after the tea she brought her and then Brenna finally fell asleep. She woke up early the next morning ready for breakfast and she came downstairs and the rest of the family had already assembled there for breakfast. The breakfast went well for the family and they prayed and asked God's blessing on the food that had been prepared as well as Brenna's wedding this evening. Her mom asked her how did she sleep and Brenna responded great and wanted to know what Leah put into her tea. She said oh nothing and smiled. Whatever it was it surely worked. Brenna knew that Julie would come and help her dress at 1:00 PM but her mom tells her don't expect Julie to come tomorrow because she has just gotten married herself. I know my friend Julie and she will be in my room at 1:00 PM. Mrs. Smaller is so proud of her daughter for saving herself or staying celibate for her husband oppose to being intimate before marriage. But mom I have heard the talk that girls repeat after they give themselves to their partner, and it's kind of frighten me. Her mom tells her that when your partner loves you the way you two love each other, he will know how to be patient and gentle with you and make it a beautiful experience that you will love with him as your marriage grows. Kids that don't know what they are doing and get into being promiscuous are the ones that have hard times dealing with the opposite sex. Actually, they should wait until marriage. This is why there are so many babies/infants out of wedlock. But Brenna I am so proud of you and I know that you will be fine and have a beautiful experience with your new husband. Mom I do love him so much and I know he loves me. That's why you don't have to worry about James. I see it in him how much he loves you. So, go get married and be happy. Yes, Mom I will and I love you so very much, and mom Smaller says and I love you too dear.

Breakfast at Brenna's house with all her immediate family went well and Julie has called Brenna to let her know that she will be at her home at 12:30 PM. Kevin is going to drop her off and make his way to James home. Julie and Kevin are so very happy when they woke up this morning. They didn't get very much sleep last night but they must be up for her friend Brenna's wedding today. She and Kevin had their very first night of sheer passion and she is still on cloud nine. Everything for her last night was just beautiful and Kevin was wonderful with her. He was so sweet. Patient and kind with her that she did not want the night to end. On waking up this morning Julie was a little uncomfortable but she smiled to herself and said just a walk in the park as long as she was with her husband. She soon forgot about it, instead she wrapped her arms around Kevin and said good morning my love. He did not hesitate to pull her close and kiss her senseless. Well we do need to get a move on before I won't let you out of here especially if you want to be at Brenna's home at 12:30. You know we will only do this for our best friends. We still have tonight and the rest of our lives together Kevin said. We will be flying out early Sunday morning for our two weeks of honeymoon the four of us. Kevin tells Julie that he is happy that the four of them are going together because they are artist and they have to be very careful not to be recognized by people in general or the public. Franklin and Arianna are in Brenna's wedding also and Franklin and Arianna are having breakfast at Brenna' home this morning. She thinks of Franklin as her brother because they were very close in college and after he met and got engage to Arianna, she also became a good friend as well. He left right after breakfast because all the guys were meeting up at the hotel to get dressed and the girls met at Brenna's to get dressed and travel to the church for the ceremony. Brenna has her two sisters Kim, and Leah in her wedding along with her maid of honor Julie and her sister Dawn, Arianna and another friend from college Kerstin Bowers. Kerstin traveled from New York City to be with her friend Brenna on her day. Alice, Camille and a few of the other friends from church agreed to usher and help out with both weddings. James sister Stephanie is singing a solo at church. Johnny's sisters are doing the programs and taking care of the church decorations.

Now Julie has arrived at Brenna's and it is time to get Brenna' hair styled and her makeup done. The stylist has done Brenna's hair now and it's her turn to get the royal treatment her makeup. The makeup artist is already at the house and is in progress with Brenna's makeup. The girls are waiting to get their makeup done as well. Mrs. Smaller has gone over to the church to make sure everything is in order for her daughter Brenna's wedding. She finds the church flowers beautifully done and in their places as requested. Mom Smaller is very pleased the way everything is being handled. She and Mrs. Summer's rushes back to get dressed so they can get ready for the ride to the church. They are two of the most fashionable and efficient women that live in Northern Atlanta area. Everyone is ready to get to the church. Brenna is absolutely stunning in her gown and her mom is crying the whole time. When they get to the church, they will have a holding space at church for the Bride and her bridesmaids to go in and relax until it's time for the wedding ceremony. The Limo has gotten to the house and Brenna her dad and mom are ready to go on over to the church. The limo truck has the wedding party along with the groomsmen. The best man is in the limo with his best friend the Groom by themselves. Kevin needed this because he needed to talk to James. He let James know that he needs to be very careful and gentle with Brenna because she is a virgin and James agreed with him. I know man and I will be on my best behavior to make it special for her. WE are getting two very special girls and can't many guys say that these days. They are in deep conversation about how nice the young ladies are and can't wait to go on their honeymoon. They get to the church and go into the Groom's space at church until the ceremony starts.

Brenna, her mom and dad arrive and they get out and Brenna goes into her Bridal space at church. Mrs. Smaller has on a deeper Lavender dress that is absolutely beautiful and she is ushered into the church and take her seat in the area until it's time for them to come into the Sanctuary. Her two little flower girls are so beautiful. They have a white dress with Dahlia ribbons around the waste, white shoes and white flower baskets with Dahlia, white and gold flowers. The ring bearer has a white tuck with Dahlia tie, suspenders and handkerchief with white shoes as well. The bridesmaids have Dahlia dresses and their bouquets are absolutely beautiful and match their dresses completely. However, Julie, the maid of honor has on a slightly darker Dahlia dress and it is absolutely stunning along with the bridesmaids. They all look gorgeous. The colors are so beautiful together. Julie said WOW when she saw the dresses and how everyone looked in them. I love your colors Brenna, and she told her that she loved her colors as well. She has to talk to Julie when they get married before they go to the honeymoon suite tonight. The Groom and his groomsmen have taken their place and the Shekinah Praise Band starts to play from the choir area and Brian stars to sing a solo for his sister Brenna. All the bridesmaids are now set to walk in and as they processed in. Brian finishes the song. One by one all the bridesmaids enter the church and take their places. Now Julie walks in as her husband Kevin is singing so beautiful a song of How God's love kept them grounded. Brenna wrote this song and had Kevin to sing it as Julie takes her place beside all the other bridesmaid. Now the runner is rolling down the aisle of the church and her two flower girls start to walk in with their baskets of flowers sprinkling petals along the center aisle of the church and then the ring bearer comes in behind the girl. Then they started to play the wedding march here comes the Bride and the entire church stood up as Brenna and her dad walk in together. Brenna is such a beautiful young lady and more stunning in her wedding dress. She walks in with dad and takes her place beside her husband to be. The minister does the ceremony and it was so beautiful. After the minister tell James you may now kiss your bride and he did just that. The minister announced them husband and wife and James whispered in her ear; you are now Mrs. James Kenneth Williams. He started down the aisle and Brenna held him back as she sang God has Smiled on me and James and Brenna had tears in their eyes when she finished. They walked out of the church into the vestibule area to shake hands with all their guest before going to the grounds of the hotel to take pictures. Their guest was received at the hotel for an hour of finger food before the reception. Brenna, James, Kevin and Julie are sent in a different direction to check out the reception area and it was spectacular. The tables were set up so nicely and the flowers was amazing on each table. The wedding planner had outdone themselves. Then they slipped back to the area to get their pictures done. James kept holding her and kissing her and the photographer was capturing all of the pictures. After an hour and fifteen minutes all pictures had been taken and the rest would be taken inside of the reception.

Their parents had been escorted into the reception area and introduced. They were standing at the door until all their bridesmaid and groomsmen had processed in, they are ready to be announced as Mr. & Mrs. James Kenneth Williams II. James kisses her again and then they made their way into the reception dancing. They had their first dance together as husband and wife and then they danced with each other's parents and the groomsmen and the bridesmaid took the floor and the reception was in full swing. James finished his dance with her and they took their seats and later on he asked her to dance and he was given a Mic as instructed by him so he could sing to his beautiful wife. This was a great reception for Brenna. Julie did get to Brenna and told her not to be afraid that it was just going to be a little uncomfortable for a little while and that she would be ok. Julie came over to Brenna before they left the reception with a cup of hot tea with Blackberry Brandy in it and Brenna felt great. It was going to be a lovely night with her now husband. She had the best time at her wedding reception and then it was over and time to go to the Honeymoon suite. Now, Brenna could not wait to get to her room, she wanted nothing more than to be with her husband. They got to their honeymoon suite it was so beautiful she did not want to turn down the bed. Everything else was kind of a blur because she was so in love with James she was out of her mind. She had her relaxing bath while James showered and prepared himself for her as well. They were so loving to each other and then it was just heaven and they did not sleep very much Friday night. James awaken her very early Saturday morning with a smile and a kiss. He kept her in bed most of Saturday morning just resting and relaxing. Brenna was a little uncomfortable but nothing she couldn't handle Brenna thought of what Julie said and she felt the same way, just a walk in the park. They ordered in and called Kevin and Julie and they did the same thing and agreed to meet them down stairs to have a cocktail later on that evening. Most of their bags were packed for the honeymoon before they left their home and they were dropping off their things that they had for the wedding at her parents' home after they had their cocktail.

The four of them boarded the plane on Sunday morning for Sandals resort in Jamaica. They stayed for a week there and then on to (DR) Dominican Republic. The four of them got such a tan and had a great honeymoon. None of them wanted to return but they knew they had their tour coming up for their first CD. They made it back to the states and they were so happy. They both rented out Condos and had them furnished before their wedding so they would have a place when they returned home. Both of the girls live in the same complex. They plan to buy homes but they will do this when they come off their tour or wait a year and see what their plans for the future are for their family.

They both want to have a baby as soon as possible. The way Brenna is feeling she may be pregnant already. So, they are going to get their tour done and see what the deal is with both of them being mothers. The four of them went directly to their Condos and noticed that they had been cleaned from top to bottom and clothes and everything was in place. Brenna knew that the two mothers had gotten together and made sure their condos was spotless when they returned. They both loved their mom's because they always had their backs. They each had maid service at their homes For the day and dinner had been prepared for them and even waited on them as they had dinner and cleaned up their kitchen and left them alone. What a blessing for them to come home and have nothing to do except eat and go to bed because they were pretty tired from the honeymoon and travel. They wouldn't have the energy if they wanted to. Brenna called Julie and told her of her good fortune only to discover that she had the same treatment at her condo. Their parents had stayed a day in their condos while their phone was being installed. Julie and Brenna had taken care of this before they left so when they returned, they would have their phones on and ready to work. Brenna and Julie brought their mom's something special from the Islands because they were so deserving of it. The guys bought the fathers a bottle back. They rented the two condos that's in the same complex and two doors down from each other. This will help out when they are working and have a problem that needs to be solves immediately, they are close enough to each other without having to get into a car and travel to the other one's home.

CHAPTER
EIGHT

Brenna and Julie just arrived back from their honeymoon. They are taking a week off to get settled into their condos. Brenna calls Julie and let her know that she is very tired and can use a few days off so she won't be going into the studio for work. James and Kevin are taking some days off themselves to relax and just enjoy their new wives of two weeks. Kevin and James meet up outside of the condos and Kevin tells James that he did not know that you could love someone so much it hurts. He truly loves Julie and hopes that they are expecting good news of a baby within the next month. James is in agreement with Kevin because he has loved Brenna since they were teenagers. No one that he has ever met held his attention the way Brenna has. He knew that Brenna was the one for him and that she was going to be his wife one day. He remembers sitting down in his grandparent's presence and telling them that he was going to marry Brenna and Mr. & Mrs. Summers just smiled because they were remembering when they were young kids in love as well and had said the same thing. They got married and their marriage seems to be a life time of love because they're still together. He was thinking of this as he talks to Kevin.

Brenna seems extra tired today and just wants to sleep in. Julie calls her and tells her that she is really tired and need a lazy day. So, they both seems to be out of it. They have been rushing around for twelve days. First in Jamaica and then in (DR) Dominican Republic. She tells Julie that she is going back to bed and Julie said to her that sounds like a good idea to me. They slept for three days, getting up long enough to eat, drink a cup of coffee and juice and shower and then go back to bed. It seems that the guys had really tired them out.

After the fourth day their mothers seemed a little concern about them and drove over to their condos to see if they were alright and how they were doing since their marriage. Neither one of them had showed up at their parents' home since their marriage and they felt a little strange with the girls not coming around and letting them know how their honeymoon was. They both had the same excuse, they're just tired from the honeymoon and traveling and site seeing. Brenna told her mom that it was just a lot to take in. The tours really were the one that tired them out because they were booked everyday to go out when they much rather had been in their hotel room. Of course, they could not tell their husbands that because they were trying to make it really good for them on their honeymoon. Which it really was but very tiring. They would have gone to the moon with them had they asked them too.

Brenna's Mom asked if she wanted her to make her some coffee or tea for her and she said sure. Then her mom tells her that she stopped at the bakery and got some breakfast rolls and Danish for her and Julie. Her phone was ringing and it was Julie calling to say that she was going to come over in five minutes for coffee and rolls. Her mom told her that they had brought them over for them and wanted them to get together for breakfast. This was a good idea and maybe this would give them some energy to get up and talk to their moms like old times in their kitchen. Their moms were eager to talk to them and ask them question and let them ask questions as well about their honeymoon if they wanted to talk about it. They were not going to push the girls if they did not want to talk. They wanted to know if the girls were alright and Brenna said to her mom yes, I am fine but the initial shock, I was not fine but James was so loving and kind which calmed me down and he was so loving and passionate that I soon forgot. It was one of the most beautiful experiences that I've ever had. Julie chimed in and said I am fine too but I knew I was in trouble when I did not know what to do and my husband was so sweet and loving in showing me how to love him and him showing me how to be loved by him. I soon understood the true meaning of loving and being loved. It was one of the greatest experiences I've ever had as well. Brenna said, I think Julie and I was so naïve to life because we had never experienced anything like it. I am truly happy that we remained celibate until we got married. I knew I loved James but now I love him even more. All young ladies should wait for their husbands before jumping into bed with them before marriage. It is so worth waiting for and I thank God every day that he gave me good sense to do so.

The girls told their mom's without going into details of their entire honeymoon, just minimal details of their trip. While they were in Jamaica at Sandals Resorts, they met one of their college friends that has relocated to Jamaica to work at Sandals Resort. The four of them were out enjoying the evening show there and they heard someone calling out to them and they spoke briefly and he asked them if they would perform a few songs for the evening and of course they did. Their first song was an upbeat Gospel song that they always do to give thanks to God for the Reverence and goodness that He has shown them and then the tempo changed to R & B which their friend did not know they could or would do since they are gospel artists. They were really good and the audience loved it and kept saying to them more, more. They explained to the audience that they were on their honeymoon and had not planned on performing while they were on leave from their group. The manager asked them if they would come back and perform for them if they give them a call later on in the year, or perhaps next year. They asked them what was the name of the group and Brenna the fast thinker said Heart & Soul. Brenna was so excited when she was explaining it to her mom and Julie's mom on how great they were and the music played by the band there for them were incredible. Her mom saw how excited and happy she was in explaining what they did and she at that moment understood her daughter fully on how she just enjoyed performing and how passionate she is about it whether its Gospel or R & B. She cannot tell her daughter not to sing R & B or Gospel. She has laid the foundation for Brenna and the best upbringing that she gave her and all her children and she know that Brenna will make the right choices in life and not stray from it. She is a young lady that has been taught morals and values of being a young lady and has to make her own choices in what she sings now. Her husband has a Christian background as well and she knows that they will be fine. Julie also expressed how excited they had been there in Jamaica when they were performing. While the four of them were there, they talked about another group of singers mainly the four of them singing R & B with the name of <u>Heart & Soul.</u> The four of them can handle this group, if they schedule the dates around the performances of Shekinah Praise tour and other appearances and not too close together. What they have to do now is think about Kevin as a Solo artist because he already has his career. This will be an ongoing discussion and see where we are with our tour for our new CD that has hit the charts while they were on their honeymoon. The group Heart & Soul has not been confirmed yet. Although they know they can sing R & B really well, this can be a life altering experience, especially since the both of them wants to have a baby within their first year of marriage. Brenna and Julie's mom reminded them that they have expressed an interest of having their first child real soon. How are you girls going to manage being pregnant and traveling around the states? When you get pregnant, there will be times when you might not feel well and you still have to get up and go away and perform. Yes, mom said Brenna & Julie, it is a lot we have to consider before we decide if we are going to commit to the R & B group. We are thinking that if we do commit to both groups, we will do minimum appearances. We want to tour with Shekinah Praise first and focus mainly on our gospel roots, and if we have the time, we will work on our R & B group. WE must go forward with our first commitment Shekinah Praise. We might even advertise or showcase for singer for the R & B group and not be selfish thinking we can do it all. Since we have the studio we can advertise and see what kind of artist we can get for this group and then manage them especially if we are pregnant. We have talked to James and Kevin and insisted on their input about the R & B group. Kevin thinks that the four of us can do this R & B group if we keep the events in the Caribbean area. This might work out but what if they are doing so well in Jamaica and their time is demanded there, then what will they do? James thinks it's a great idea to just have their manager which is Brenna and Terrence to get as many dates and appearance they can for the states to keep Shekinah Praise busy. Brenna's mom is still concern about the girls getting pregnant and running around in their first trimester. The moms don't want their daughters to lose their babies. They want them to stay healthy as possible. Mrs. Smaller did not have trouble with any of her pregnancies but no two people are alike. She stressed this to Brenna and so did Mrs. Glass. Julie's mom said it seems like you girls really had a great time and we are going to leave you to your own devices today. We are just going to run along and stop at the mall and pick up a few items, so we will see you all at the church on Sunday or later on in the week.

Brenna is wide awake and has picked up some energy from the visit and so has Julie. Do you feel up to going to the studio around 1:00 today, Julie asked and Brenna, responded well maybe, but I think James wants a lazy evening and I promised him that I would take this week to just spend with him and not go in to the studio. You know I promised Kevin the same thing and here we are planning to go into the studio and not keep our word to them. I think we should just stay home as we promised them, we would do and get some rest and they looked at each other and smiled thinking what rest are we going to get with these guys around. They continued to talk and they heard them as they got near the door and James came in and Julie asked where was Kevin and he replied that he is going to your place. Julie opened the door and called out to Kevin, hey babe come on over to Brenna's for coffee and a roll. Kevin got there in record time. I thought you was going to get some rest; she smiled and gave him a big kiss and a hug. So, Kevin asked what was we up too and Brenna said they had been talking to their mom about their performance in Jamaica and they did not form any opinion on what we should do. They told us that we are young women now and old enough to make grown up decisions and if they can't make them, come and talk to them again and they will give their opinion and see what they think of it. Brenna asked James and Kevin what they think about the R & B group as a whole moving forward in the secular rheum. Julie is kind of worried about the pressure it will put on Kevin as a Solo artist and then sometime still performing with Shekinah Praise. She thinks it will be a challenge for him as well as exhausting himself to a point that will make him ill. Kevin chimes in and say that if it becomes too much, he will not perform with Shekinah Praise at all. He will only have limited performance with them as it is and he doesn't think this will be a problem unless the Holy Spirit moves within the group and then it might be exhausting. However, when I am singing for Jesus, it is never too much. I think I can focus on my career as a Solo artist and then work with the group as well. James is thinking the same thing about his wife Brenna working as the manager for both Kevin and then Shekinah Praise and then performing with Shekinah and now they are talking about this R & B group. If this new group becomes a reality, this is more stress on her especially if they are trying to get pregnant. James already thinks Brenna is pregnant because she has been so tired and sleepy this week. This is the third week and the end of next week he'll insist that she go to the doctor for a checkup. He has talked to Kevin about it and he feels the same way about Julie. They will know for sure next week because they will insist the girls see a doctor. James has already called an OBGYN and made an appointment for Brenna to come in and told Kevin and he called the same OBGYN and made an appointment for Julie and they are coming in the same day around the same time next Friday. They want the girls to get a complete physical before they go out on the road as well as themselves. They all want to be fit for this tour because it is ten weeks and they are doing two to three cities a week. This is a lot for new artist but since they have been doing concerts for the last year, they feel that they can handle it for their new CD and everyone needs to be healthy. They will know for sure next week if the girls are both pregnant.

Well the girls are very happy with their husbands taking real good care of them. Brenna & Julie both are getting sleepy and Kevin says to Julie come on sleepy head I have to get you home for some much-needed rest. Julie looks at Brenna and they both know what that comment meant. They are both smiling to themselves because they both need to be with their husbands now. Kevin & Julie says good bye and walks out of the condo. Brenna could hardly wait for them to close the door, before they ran into each other's arms and head upstairs to their bedroom. Their love for each other is so strong and their intimacy is exquisite. It was so passionate that they could not let each other go for a minute. He held her so close and told her how much he loved and needed her. She did not move from his arms until later on in the evening. She was totally exhausted from her mom and Julie's mom coming over and then entertaining Julie and her husband coming together with them to discuss the decision they have to make regarding the new group that they are planning on implementing. Brenna just felt like loving her husband in every way all afternoon. She never knew that being married to James could be so sweet and wonderful but it's a blessing for the both of them. This is real love. Hey babe said Brenna to James, let's go to bed, I'm tired.

It is Friday the day of their appointment to go to the doctors and the girls are wondering how they got the appointment so fast but it was because of their husbands calling their moms to find out about an OBGYN. They told their moms that they wanted the girls to have their checkup before going out on the road and their moms agreed that this was a good idea. Julie goes in and gets her examine and the doctor gives her a pregnancy test and it came out positive and she and Kevin are all smiles and they don't say anything until Brenna goes in and gets her examine and takes the pregnancy test. Hers was positive as well. Boy Brenna is so excited and trying to contain herself. When she and James come out, they come over and sit with Kevin and Julie and the two of them are smiling from ear to ear and so was Brenna and James. So, what is the verdict, they say we're pregnant and Brenna says so are we. Doctor Moore knows how close the four of them are and calls them into his conference room to talk to them about their tour. He lets them know that the girls have to be especially careful in their first trimester, not to get too stressed out and lose their babies. They must get as much rest as possible and not be doing or lifting anything too heavy. They must take care to have an easy pregnancy. James said, that's it you are no longer the manager for any group now. You will be taking care of yourself and our baby. We will talk to Terrence and Kevin's brother Michael about taking over the manager's job for Shekinah Praise and Kevin the Artist until after the baby is born. Kevin's brother Michael has been training under Brenna to be a manager for Kevin and Terrence can do Shekinah Praise. Brenna had forgotten that Alice had called her before she left on their honeymoon that she is already two months pregnant with her second child. Oh, my goodness I forgot that Alice is already pregnant said Brenna. At least she will be out of her first trimester when they go on tour. My goodness three babies in the group. She was so happy that she forgot to mention to Julie, James and Kevin. When she told them, they were happy and when they get home, they would call Terrence and Alice to come over the weekend to celebrate with a cookout at Julie's parent's house this time. They have so much to be thankful for right now. Two months later, the guys are driving over to Brenna's parents' house to give them the good news. When they arrive at Mr. & Mrs. Smaller's house they walk in and Brenna goes straight to the kitchen to see what is there to eat. She misses her mom's great cooking. Mrs. Smaller calls Mrs. Summers to come over and bring her husband and call the rest of Julie's family, Mrs. Glass and her husband and Julie's siblings about the tour. They wanted to keep this a surprise until the families are all together. They are coming over thinking they are going to discuss the tour but they are going to be in for a big surprise with the news that they have. Mrs. Summers called Johnny and Camille to come over as well. The two of them are now engaged. After all the three families has gathered, Brenna, James, Julie, and Kevin have discussed how they are going to tell them all. James and Kevin will give the news to the families. James stands and then Kevin Stands and says that the tour news is that Brenna and Julie both are expecting babies in the spring. Everyone was shocked because they did not know that it would be this soon. They knew they wanted to have children right away but they did not know they meant now! After The initial shock has worn off, they came up and congratulated the guys and gave the girls a big hug and wished them the best. Then both moms asked nearly at the same time what about the tour and will you be going in another week and they answered yes but they will be very careful not to lift or do anything that will be detrimental to their babies and their health. They promised they would be getting more sleep and Terrence and Kevin's brother Michael will be managers until the girls give birth. They may not ever take the managers jobs back depending on how much it will be on the girls after giving birth. Kevin has another brother Trey Alan Snow, that maybe they can convince to come down to Atlanta and work with them also for a while. They are not sure on this one because he is running the studio for his father back in Syracuse, NY. His dad has other family members that is working there and perhaps Trey can be on loan until the birth of Julie's Baby or maybe they can send another family member to help out. Kevin tells them he will put in a call to his mom and dad when they get home to discuss a few things about the upcoming tour. Brenna and Julie's fathers says this calls for a toast and they brought out a bottle of Brandy to celebrate. The mothers are in tears and the girls are trying to console them and letting them know that they will be fine and not to worry about them. Brenna's sisters Kim and Leah are so happy, but they are watching their mom get really emotional and they rushed over to her to let her know that they won't let anything happen to Brenna. Brenna is the youngest daughter and everyone in the family have been very protective of her because she almost died when she was three years old. When they told this to James, he got emotional himself because he had never heard this story before. He loves her so much and he thanks God every day for her. Julie's parents are emotional as well because she is also the youngest in her family as well. Her sister and brother are so happy for Julie and Kevin Snow. The girls have been best friends since they were eleven years old. Then the two of them stood up and said to the families that its ok and they will be ok and will watch out for each other and will not overdo it. They will go back to the doctor in their third month to see how the babies are growing and to make sure they are taking their prenatal vitamins and in good health. All the family members are so excited because this will be the first babies born in both their families in twenty-one years. Well we are going to go home and Kevin has asked his in-laws if they could have a get together for the entire Shekinah Praise group on Sunday afternoon so they can make the announcement to the group and everyone will be on the same page. Brenna stood and said that there will be three babies being born into the group in the spring. Brenna said that Alice has already informed us that she is having a baby before we left on our honeymoon. With all the excitement of my marriage to James I forgot to mention it and Alice did not want to say anything about herself to take away from the girls' weddings. Julie's mom said that this was so sweet of Alice to think of the girls oppose to herself. They are now seeing a side of Alice that they really like, now that they are all good friends and singing together. She and Terrence has become great friends in the group as well. Everyone gets along just fine now.

The tour starts in two weeks and they have to be ready for it. All their outfits should be ready and packed. Brenna and Julie's mom are now helping out with the wardrobe/fashions for the girls for this tour. They have help from their older daughters and cousins that want to be part of the business. One of the cousins is a fashion designer and has been supplying them with the latest styles for the group. She has opened up a shop in downtown Atlanta and the shop is flourishing. They have been giving them all the business because they have all the latest styles for young artist. They fly in to New York and LA for clothes for the girls and the guys. The three pregnant girls will be just fine with all the large fashion tops they are wearing now. They will be right in style for them. Their cousin Violet Smaller has been doing so well that she expanded her shop so she can accommodate the entertaining artist. She has beautiful fitting rooms for Artist to come in and get clothing without tripping over people. The entertainment side of the store is basically for people in the industry. The other side of the store, is strictly for fashions for consumers. Sometimes Violet visits the artist home to accommodate them when they don't want to come into the store or don't have the time. However, it's challenging but this is more money for her and she loves doing this for her clients and her family. She has given Shekinah Praise a day to come in after hours to get fitted for their attire for touring. Shekinah Praise is not being charged when she visits their home at all because it's family. Violet has given them great discounts because the family has helped her get to where she is today. Without their help she would be still struggling. She loves her family and will help them to no end because of what they did for her and they told her that she did not have to return anything to them.

That's what family is all about. Now she is paying it forward. She has all of her siblings working for her and they are doing it to make the business great. She has been giving a scholarship to a student every year for the last three years since she has opened up the shop. She says her auntie Ella and uncle George encouraged her to do this to help a less fortunate student and she would be blessed for it. She knows without a doubt that she is blessed for her business is souring for it. Violet will be visiting Julie's home for the announcement of the babies. She has heard through the immediate family but now they are announcing it to everyone that is a part of the family and friends. She has a manager in place for the afternoon to make sure all her clients are taken care of in the manner they are accustomed to. She takes her business real serious and will leave from her family's home if a problem arises and return back to her place of business to take care of the problem. There is no shame in what she is all about. Auntie Ella and uncle George has taught her really well how to run a business and stay in the game.

It is Saturday and everyone has gathered at the Summer's home for the pool party, and outdoor cook out. All of Shekinah Praise is here as well as Kevin's parents, the Snow's. They flew in from Syracuse, NY for the announcement of their first grandbaby of Kevin and Julie Snow and the first grandbaby of the Smaller's, Brenna and James Williams baby. They are all so very happy right now. Alice and Terrence are there with her parents and her in-laws for the announcement also of their second grandchild of the Blacks. Brenna and Julie are in their 2nd month and Alice is in her third month. Also, the grandparents made the announcement about Johnny and Camille of their marriage in the Spring. Johnny looked directly at Julie when the announcement was made. Brenna is not sure what the stare was all about with him. She kind of sauntered around to James to go and question him as to what's up with him and Julie. He made his decision when he broke off their relationship and he still have a grudge about Julie and Kevin. He needs to get over it already because Julie is married and expecting Kevin's baby and they are very happy right now.

Everyone is either in the pool or standing around wishing Franklin and Arianna well on their upcoming nuptials late October. This will happen right after the tour. This will make for a better tour as everyone will be married or getting married and no upsets about who's talking to whom and seeing another person. It is the second week in August and they leave on tour on Monday. Their first tour stop is Syracuse, NY, at the theater there, and then on to Buffalo, NY the next day. The first tour stops in Syracuse, Brenna hit the stage and boy did she bring it. She was on a spiritual high. In Buffalo they had raised their performance to another level and it was fantastic. Julie performed like she had never performed before. Kevin performed with them for this tour and he brought the house down. Four days later at the Theater on Sunday in Rochester they left everything out on the stage. They hit New Jersey a few days later. From there they are in Washington, DC, Virginia, North Carolina, South Carolina, Ohio, Chicago. Illinois, Kentucky, Tennessee, Texas, Kansas, Arkansas, Mississippi, Florida, Louisiana and then back home to Georgia. Every performance was on a different level. They have almost three stops in each state. They planned a trip to California to one of Kevin's father's friend's church. A man that Kevin calls Uncle Jerry Miller. This concert was different because Kevin performed as the Solo artist with his backup singers. Kevin's background singers never missed a beat. It was like they were all still performing together. The tour was very good and very uplifting for the girls and they did not tire themselves out at all. Their husbands made them take care and take naps when they weren't performing. So, they stayed rested up. They would go in for sound check and never stayed any longer than two hours to make sure everything was working fine. They checked in with their parents with good reports every two days. Alice seems to have more problems than they did but she was gaining more weight than they were because she was going into her fifth month. She did not perform with them for a few weeks of the concert because the doctor wanted her to stay off her feet for a few days and rest and the girls made her do it and Kim stepped in and helped out with her songs. No one ever knew the difference. The last few days Terrence, had his mom fly in and get Alice and fly her back home. The tour was getting to be too much for her. When they got back to Georgia, she rejoined the group but no more traveling for her until after the baby is born unless they are in the immediate area. Terrence told her that it was his and the Doctors orders and she must follow them or she was not performing any more until after the baby comes. She was not going to put her little girls' life in danger. She had found out that she was having a girl. She was jumping for joy but not happy that she could not perform. It was so funny telling their audience that they all were pregnant and their husbands was making sure they did not overdo it.

Their tour is completed and they are back home in North Atlanta until December. The girls are going to the doctors for their three-month checkup today and they can hardly wait. Both of them have a little pot belly. Brenna is showing just a little more than Julie but Julie is built different and Brenna is concerned that she is gaining too much weight. James told her that she is fine and don't worry about it. Well when they get into the Doctors office, they did not see Dr. Jerry Miller only Dr. Moore and Dr Jones. Dr. Jones looks at Brenna and say wow you gain a little bit of weight there and this upsets Brenna and the doctor says to her don't be so concerned, it could be just you're retaining a bit more water than usual but let's see what is going on here. I will take you first today Brenna and how did the tour go? Brenna begin to tell her how wonderful it was and the guys made sure they got plenty of rest and stayed off their feet when they were not performing. Brenna, I want you on the table and James I want you to take a seat so you can see the Sonogram and hear the heartbeat of the baby. He sits and the doctor tells him to pick up the stethoscope to hear the baby's heartbeat. Oh, my goodness this is unbelievable. Then she tells him to take a look at the screen and she says oh wait a minute I hear two heart beats and I see two babies. Oh, Brenna twins. She can see a little boy and oh look it appears to be a girl as well. Dr Jones says she will have to wait until Brenna gets a little larger and they can see the other baby clearly. James is shocked and so is Brenna. Then James remembered that his mom is a twin, and he tells the doctor my mother was a twin. Brenna is so overwhelmed with joy that she starts to cry and James has to hold her in his arms and console her for a few minutes. Julie hears all of the commotion in the room that she asks Kevin to come see what it's all about and he pokes his head in and that's when he sees Brenna crying and ask her if the baby is ok and that she will be alright. She looks at Kevin and says its twins and he is overjoyed and goes back over to Julie. Brenna is just so excited that she was crying. Oh, my goodness, I should go into her and Kevin tells her no you are on the bed and you are next to be examined so you stay put and she will tell you all about it when she comes out. Julie is back in the waiting room waiting on Kevin. Dr Jones tells Julie that you are in top shape and right where you need to be. Julie is so nervous about the sonogram. Kevin is listening to the baby' heart beat and then to his amazement he hears also a second heart beat and sees two babies. What is this we do everything together and at the same time. Julie is puzzled at this statement and decides to ask Kevin about this later. We are having a boy and it appears a girl. They are not sure it's a girl, they'll have to wait on this for the next Sonogram or until she gets a little bigger to see clearly what the sex of the baby is. Kevin never told Julie that he was a twin. His twin brother was stillborn. Kevin tells Julie that he himself was a twin and she held him as he cried and hugged her. God has truly blessed the four of us. The doctor tells Julie to get dressed and come out to the waiting room with Brenna and James. They were her last patients so she steps into the waiting room and tells all four of them congratulation on the twins. Brenna looks at Julie and say you are having twins and she says yes and she pipes in that they are both having twins and Dr Jones says you certainly are. What a miracle this is and our parents will never believe this in a million years. Two best friends having twins. Yes, I worked very hard on this said James but I forgot my mother was a twin. I knew Brenna was pregnant after our first night of being married. I felt the love and what we shared that night was so special. They leave Doctor Jones office together and go out to have dinner and talk about this. Out of James mouth, this is certainly going to put a halt on Shekinah Praise until after the Spring. We will continue to do concerts in the area but when it comes to traveling out of the Atlanta area for appearances and tours it will have to wait until July of next year. The R & B group is certainly out of the question and going on the Back Burner unless they interview other artist for this group. This is just a thought right now. They will table this discussion until later on. Boy we are going to need nannies said Julie and two of them at least. Four babies? I cannot wrap my head around this yet. As Brenna is talking, she is rubbing her abdomen and James takes his hand and place it on her abdomen too and say we are going to take care of you guys. He then kisses Brenna and tells her how much he loves her. I knew you was pregnant the third week of our marriage. You stayed too sleepy and you never did that. Kevin said the same thing that Julie was always sleepy and at first, I thought it was the trip until I saw how tired she was in the mornings. I knew Julie was pregnant, I was just waiting on confirmation from Dr. Jones. Julie goes how did you know that? Because I kept you pretty busy replied Kevin and I did not use protection because I want kids with you right away. James and Kevin said together we knew that we had gotten the two of you pregnant and we are so happy and pleased that our wives are carrying our babies. After they had dinner, they decided to go to their in-laws', home to tell them the good news. But to tell them together they will have to meet at one of the homes together. Kevin and Julie went to the Glass's house to give them the news and to call his parents from there. When they got there, her mom wanted to know what was the good news and they told them to have a seat first so they could explain and right away Julie's mom started to cry and Julie said Mom its good news, however it's very good news for the family. Kevin and Julie said together mom, dad we are having twins. Her mom was just smiling and so excited and wanted to know when will the babies be born and what is their gender? We know one is a boy and the other one looks like a girl but they kept moving and they could not get the sex of the second baby. Kevin said he has to call his parents and let them know as well and Julie's mother handed him the phone. He called his mom and right away. His mom asked how was Julie and the baby and Kevin said mom are you sitting down and she said I can be and found a seat on the sofa. Mom and dad, we are having twins and his mother screamed and said oh my goodness. Kevin remember I told you that you were a twin and we lost your twin brother. This is a blessing for you and Julie. Now tell me what is the sex of the babies. One is a boy and the other one we couldn't get to see because she or he kept moving but we will find out the next time we go to the doctors. How is Brenna doing with her pregnancy? You won't believe this either, Brenna is caring twins as well. James mother was a twin, and his mother said "WOW". This is so weird. I never knew that his mom was a twin. Both of them and their husbands were killed by a drunken driver. Oh, my goodness I am so sorry about that. Mom this happened when James was eleven years old. Well we will talk to you all later on in the week., bye mom and dad and I love you all, bye. Kevin and Julie. As James is pulling up into Brenna's family's drive way, she asked James what do you think mom and dad will say. They can't say anything but we love you. They get out and knock and enter the house as Brenna still has her home key. Hi mom and dad we came over to talk to you about the doctor's visit. I was wondering where you all were after the doctor's visit? Well we went out to dinner because the girls were hungry. Where is Julie? Mom asked and Brenna answered her saying she went home so we could talk to you and dad alone. Is there something wrong with the baby Brenna? Oh no mom, maybe you should sit for this one. You two what is wrong and you are scaring me. Mom, dad we are having twins. We did not see this coming and we are so happy that we get one each. Now dad can hold one and I can hold the other one. Do you know the sex of the babies? We know one is a boy and we think the other one is a girl but we couldn't get a good view of her because she kept moving. The Doctor said it looks like it's a girl from what she could see. And you would not guess this one in a million years mom, Julie is pregnant with twins as well. The baby boy is hiding the other baby and they could not see the sex of the other baby real good, but Dr Jones said it looks like a girl too. We did not know that Kevin was a twin until the doctor asked him did twins run in his family and he told us then that he was a twin but his twin brother was still born. James had forgotten that his mom was a twin so we both were really surprised o know that we will be giving birth to two babies instead of one. I will call Mary Glass tomorrow morning to congratulate her on becoming a grandma twice. You girls outdone yourselves this time. Its late mom and I want to get home and get some rest. I am very tired and sleepy lately. Yes, this is what happens when you get pregnant. The guys already told us that after the tour that we would be cutting back on the concert that we are doing especially since they are having twins. They go home to their Condo and prepare for their last concert in December. Nothing scheduled pass December because of the ice storms that they have in Georgia and they did not want anything to happen to their wives trying to get to concerts and making rehearsals. They will be taking over the running of the Studio until the girls are back on their feet. Kevin, James, Johnny and Terrence can make sure things happen there. The girls can take this time to write material for their next CD and upcoming tours and performances in the summer.

CHAPTER
NINE

Shekinah Praise Babies

Shekinah Praise did three concerts in December and what a blast they had. The first one they had was downtown Atlanta and the place was jammed packed with people coming out to hear their new CD. When the host came on the stage to announce them, they came out with one of their more popular songs on the CD. Everyone was moving to the beat and singing along with them as they performed. Brenna took the mic and boy did she take it to another level. She was on a spiritual high and James was watching her and making sure that she was not in any danger of falling or getting too hot and passing out on stage. He is still singing and walks over and takes the mic from her and finishes out the song and then tell the audience that he has to take care of his wife because she is expecting not one baby but two and she need to take it a little easier. I know my wife likes to sing and praise the Lord and I want her to do just that but I need her to be careful as well. Everyone laughed and clapped all at the same time. James continues to talk and let the audience know not only is his wife pregnant with twins, so is her friend Julie, who is pregnant and also her friend Alice. We have two of the wives pregnant with twins and another one pregnant with a little girl. So, we have to step in sometime to let them know that they are not super women just our wives, whom we love very much. Then James starts to sing and finishes one verse and gives the mic to

Kevin and he bring the house down. This is a song that he wrote for Shekinah Praise and he sings it like heaven is waiting to take them right in. He talks about his wife Julie singing and being also pregnant with twins, we don't quite know how that happen the twin part however James and I are two of the luckiest men on earth. Brenna could not contain herself and takes another mic and sang a few lines and walks center stage and took it to another level. This concert blew everyone's mine. Alice sang her song and it was so beautiful and just what the audience needed at that time. Terrence her husband walks by her side and they finish it as a duet. He also expressed that his wife is pregnant with a little girl and is further along than her friends. She has to be careful because her baby is due in February. I am a blessed man and we already have a two-and-a-half-year-old son. But God can carry you through things unimaginable. So, we thank God for the blessing. So, don't forget our Christmas Concert coming up at Emmanuel Baptist church for the Holidays.

Following their last concert, one is scheduled in three days and the last one is the Christmas concert at their church which they do every year to give back to the community. Three days has passed and it is time for them to go on stage and everyone is waiting for them to come out. As they are walking out the crown goes insane and Brenna walks to the mic and start to get the crowd worked up for the concert. Let's give God some praise up in here and tonight Shekinah Praise come to praise him. Have you come to Praise the Lord tonight and everyone is on their feet clapping and singing with them? Brenna knows this is going to be a beautiful concert because they have already set the tone for it. She sings her new song that she wrote for her and James, God is our Comfort Zone and he starts the song and they get into it and Brenna and James finishes up the duet and Terrence and Alice sing together her song that he wrote for her. Now the crowd is going crazy as they are really getting on a spiritual high. Kevin and Julie come on and do their song and the people are in a frenzy as every song they sing gets on a spiritual high. So, they bring it down some by singing a slower version of a song that is just so beautiful and sweet. James come out again and takes the mic and tell the crowd that he has to slow the pace down because they have three pregnant ladies that has to take it easy and not get too exhausted. Praise God now our wives are adding to our Shekinah Praise family and we want them to perform at least two more concerts before they go on maternity leave. We have to stop them sometime because they swear, they are super women and don't get tired of praising the Lord. We know this is true but we have to take care of them when they don't want to listen. My wife tells me all the time God's got this and I know he does but I want her to understand that when she goes home, I want her to be able to get some rest too and not be so exhausted. When she doesn't rest, I don't rest. The crown claps and laughs. My darling wife Brenna is also expecting twins in the spring and we are so excited about the babies. We went into the Doctors thinking that we were having a baby that turned out to be two babies. We want you all to know that we love you and appreciate you all for supporting us and following us on twitter, face book and our website. There are tons of our new CD's in the lobby and you can pick them up on the way out. Kevin come up front and tell our audience about your new CD. Kevin is one of our members that has a solo career as well and it is soaring as well. We love our brother dearly and we want everyone to continue to support him. We are all family and we tour together because his wife is my wife's best friend. Good evening everyone and thanks for your support for Kevin the Artist. We all met up in college singing for the Lord and after graduation we decided to go professional and see where it would lead us in the Lord. We are a blessed group of performers that loves singing and praising the Lord and we are not ashamed to do so. God has given me this voice and I will use it for him to the best of my ability. We could be doing other things in our lives but we chose to sing for the Lord. I thank God every day for keeping me and giving me my beautiful wife of five months and now she is expecting twins in the spring. I met this group of singers that was already singing in college and from what my wife tells me they started at home in their church and continued through our college days. This is amazing because you don't find this kind of commitment with young people today. When I met her, I couldn't take my eyes off of her and finally one day she agreed to go out to dinner with me and the rest is history. Well we have two more songs for tonight that we will be singing by my friends and brothers in Christ Johnny Williams and his fiancé Camille and Minister Franklin and his fiancé Arianna. They sang with such powerful voices that everyone in the place just stood up and was praising God and clapping and singing along with them. This was an awesome concert and they will forever be grateful to their audience. Well you can catch us at our home church during the Christmas holidays. This concert is for the community and we want to see each and every one of you there. Kim sings her song and she just gave the performance of her life and she got a standing ovation for it. Brenna takes the mic and let the audience know that Kim is her sister and be on the lookout for greater things coming from Kim within the next few months. Brenna's mind is already thinking of another Solo artist from their group. She has been pushing Kim to do this because she knows that her sister is really gifted with a great voice and can handle a solo career.

It is ten days before the Christmas holidays and the girls have done their shopping by going out early in the mornings before the other consumers are out and about. This way they avoided the crowd and was back home with their husbands. The guys always accompanied the girls to make sure they did not exhaust themselves out. James and Kevin hired a company to come in and decorate their condos for the Christmas holidays and both homes looked very festive. After the holidays they will take down the decorations. After the holidays the company will come in and take down the decorations. Well, the girls had one morning where they just wanted to go out with their mothers to get gifts for their husbands and purchase items for the twins as well as their siblings. They will be purchasing their cribs and other furniture for the baby's room during January when everything is on sale and if not, they will send out their fashion patrol to purchase it for them. They know who that will be, their mom's. Around two o'clock in the afternoon they are going into the studio to rehearse their songs for the Christmas concert. Their husbands will only let them stay two hours and they have to leave. Terrence has stopped Alice from going all together. So, one day out of the week we go over to their house to go over the songs with her. She is only going to sing with Terrence and sit out in the audience because she is too near her time for delivery. James and Kevin have to go see Pastor so they can get prepared for the concert at the church. They are only preparing six songs because the church choir will also sing and will sing a few songs with Shekinah Praise. Pastor calls and tells Brenna that he is on cloud nine waiting for this concert to happen. They know the Christmas songs that will be performed. What they plan to do is record their Christmas concert at church and the CD they recorded in August for the Holidays will be out during the Holidays season. Shekinah Praise had been recording these songs back in August and the CD will hit the stores Thanksgiving week. This CD should flood the market around the Thanksgiving holidays leading up to Christmas. The name of the CD is Christmas with Shekinah Praise.

All the lights in the neighborhood and city limits are really beautiful, reflecting the Christmas Holiday season. Everyone seemed to have gone out and bought extra lights to make their yards more beautiful. Brenna's mom had her landscaping people to hang lights for them and most of their neighbors used them as well to make their yards beautiful too. They really mad it very special and beautiful. You could see people driving up and down the street to see all the beautiful lights and admire and even take pictures of the area.

It is the day of the concert and Shekinah Praise is hyped up and ready to perform. They are all dressed in their shimmering gold flared dress with black and gold corsages and men in their black tucks, white shirts and gold ties and gold boutonniere in their jacket collar lapel. The Choir is dressed in long flowing black skirts and gold blouses with back and gold corsages and the guys with black suits white shirts and gold ties and gold handkerchief in jacket pocket. The entire church is decorated so beautifully to match the holiday season. Everything is just lovely. Now as everyone is in place and Brenna is coming out onto the open choir loft and directing the choir to take their places. Brenna takes the MIC as she is the MC for the evening along with Julie, James and Johnny. This is their home church and they come to represent. The choir is directed to stand and perform and Julie, James, Johnny and Brenna stand along with the choir and perform a couple of songs with them as Kevin directs. Then they bowed out and relax on the side until it is time for Shekinah Praise to perform. The Choir came on to perform the rest of the songs. They had been working with Shekinah Praise for a few weeks since their director had major surgery. The choir was extremely good and everyone was up on their feet clapping and shouting when they had finished. Julie whispered to Brenna that they are good enough to record and Brenna said she was thinking of that. Brenna will let the choir know that they have an offer to make to the church but they don't want the choir to know that they want to give them an opportunity to record their songs. This will be a Christmas blessing to them on behalf of Brenna and Julie's Studio. That will be a project for them to work on when they come off maternity leave. It is time for Shekinah Praise to return back to the open choir loft for their performance. Brenna is given the MIC and she walks out front and center and ask how is everyone doing tonight? I am fine Glory to God just a little heavier than before and she got a few laughs from the audience. We are here tonight to celebrate the birth of our Lord and Savior Jesus Christ. We are so happy to be home and to perform in our home church. We have just finished our first tour as professional singers, Praise God, and the name of our group is Shekinah Praise and our Christmas CD has already been released and you can purchase it at any of the musical stores in the area. It was released the day after Thanksgiving. We even have them back stage after the concert is over. See any of our people out in the vestibule area. We are a Blessed group of singers that loves singing for the Lord to let our light shine that others may see. Our first song tonight is Mary Did you know and they had rearranged all of the Christmas songs that they sang. Really, they were great songs that had been arranged for Shekinah Praise. Everyone was up on their feet clapping and singing with Shekinah Praise. Brenna had taken her song to another level and out of the corner of her eye she saw James move toward her and finishes the song for her. He pauses and let the church audience know that his wife is expecting twins and needs to take it easy. She responds that she does get a little crazy when she's singing for Jesus and she knows that he will take care of her but she must listen to her husband. My sister Kim is singing this next song and we know that you will enjoy it. Kim performs and everyone is up on their feet too. Right after Kim Alice and Terrence does a Christmas duet that he has written and then Julie & Kevin brings down the house with Bethlehem. Johnny and Camille sings then Franklin and Arianna sang and Franklin literally preached and it was people shouting and praising God like never before. Well it's nearing the end of the concert and Pastor comes up and take the MIC and asked James if Brenna could sing his favorite song and he nods yes. I know how it is when your husband tells you that you have to take care of yourself and you don't listen. All I want her to do is sing just one verse and the course and I am just blessed for the night. Brenna gets the MIC and she sings like she never sang it before; she was awesome and the entire church was rocking all over again. Finally, the concert was over and Julie, Brenna and Alice really needed to get home and go to bed. They really had fun performing but they were worn out. This was Alice's last concert with Shekinah Praise until she gives birth. Alice looks like she's having twins herself but she's further along than Brenna and Julie.

Christmas day at Brenna's mom and dad's home was filled with so much joy and laughter. Julie's in-laws will be flying in on Christmas day late in the evening because they didn't want Julie flying into Syracuse or being on her feet traveling this far along in her pregnancy. Everyone is flying into Atlanta for Christmas. Kevin's parents made it in without any trouble or delays. They will be flying back in five days. Terrence is planning a New Year 's, Eve party at his house for his wife because he doesn't want Alice out and about near her delivery date but he wanted her friends around her at this time because she had been so emotional lately and when she is around the girls, she seems to be happy. So, it is New Year's Eve and the entire staff of Shekinah Praise with their significant other was invited to Alice and Terrence's house. The food had been catered and everything was really beautiful. Brenna's & Julie's parents had suggested that Alice and Terrence use the caterer that they use for the Holidays because the food was very good and they had done that. Their parents made a brief appearance because of Shekinah Praise and they went home fairly early because they had guest from out of town and a party of their own piers and friends were at their home.

The party for Terence and Alice was great and they really enjoyed themselves with the entire group and a few of their friends. They stayed there with Alice and Terrence until 2:30 AM and then everyone left. When Brenna and James arrived home, she was all hyped up and James had her to sit down so she could unwind and calm down. Brenna and Julie are always hyped whenever they do a concert and it takes a lot to calm them down. Brenna has to realize that she is caring twins and need all the rest she can get. James made her a glass of warm milk. This seems to soothe her and then she is ready to go to bed. She goes and takes a shower while he's getting the milk and all is ready for her when she comes out in her robe, she drinks the milk and eat a cookie and then she goes and brush her teeth and go back and wait for him to get out of the shower. He comes out he goes over to Brenna and picks her up and takes her to their bedroom. God, she loves her husband so much. He seems to always know just what she needs. The minute they hit the bed they are in each other's arms. He shows her just how much he loves her. After a while, they are still in each other's arms facing each other, the babies are really moving around and then James felt a kick from the babies. Oh, my goodness they kicked me, exclaimed James and he begins to laugh and tells Brenna they are telling him to go to sleep and leave mommy alone. I can't wait for them to get here so that I can take care of them. I've always wanted to have children of my own and soon we will have them. I really love you so much Brenna and are you comfortable now, if not I will get you more pillars if you feel you need them. Oh, honey as long as you are here beside me, I am fine. I love it when you say things like that and then he kisses her again. Now go to sleep so one of us will be rested by morning. You know Brenna out of all of this I did not think of my mother being a twin and it was totally amazing to know that that we are having twins and my mother's genes came out in our babies. She is not here with me, but my babies will live on through her God's willing. James raises both his hands in a prayer like position and says, thank you Lord God and thank you mommy.

Kevin and Julie are at their town house and he's rubbing Julie's feet and abdomen as the babies are moving and squirming around and Kevin is just fascinated over all of this. He had forgotten that he was a twin until he was at the doctor's office and the doctor told them they were having twins. Julie and Kevin are so excited about the babies. They like James and Brenna are having a boy and a girl too. These babies will always be close friends. We will raise them to be best friends just like Brenna and Julie and Kevin and James.

They are two of the happiest couples living in the Atlanta area. Brenna and James are now fast asleep and Kevin and Julie are just relaxing in bed and kind of drifting off to sleep. As they awake the next morning, Brenna says she wants to relax in for a few hours before she ventures out to her mom and dad's house. She goes over to her Mom and Dad's house and James will pick her up after they have dinner. They will walk across the street to James grandparent's home for dessert. They both love their parents so much. Even though James lost his parents he thinks of his grandparents as his parents because they raised him and his cousins. For Holidays they spend equal time with both. Sometimes they meet up at their home and both the parents and grandparents are there because they are all close friends and now family.

Kevin's parents are leaving the middle of the week to be home for Service on Saturday evening for New Year's Eve and Sunday New Year's Day. Mr. Snow is planning on retiring at the end of the year and his son is stepping up to become the next pastor of his church. Rev. Snow Senior will only be on the board of his recording company.

James and Brenna arrive at their parents for dinner and stay for a few hours and they walk to James grandparent's home for dessert. Brenna is feeling a little stressed and tired today, but she has been crazy busy with the group and performing. She just needs to go to bed a little earlier tonight and rest more the next few days, however they did stop in at her in-law's' home for dessert and coffee and spend almost two hours with them as well. James sees that Brenna is yawning and looking sleepy and gets up and hugs his grandparents and tells them that its time that Brenna get home and get some much-needed rest. They stop briefly at Julie's parents because they live generally in the vicinity of each other. When they get to the Glasses house Julie is sitting very quietly as her parents are engaged in a conversation with her in-laws who are staying at Julie's parents until Wednesday. Mr. Snow and his wife will travel back down on New Year's Day to be with Kevin and Julie and her parents again, leaving the following Tuesday to get back to Syracuse, NY. Brenna and Julie will be having their babies the end of March or earlier because they are both caring twins. Real coincident that this happen the way it did. They both are taking time off from the Studio to spend quality time with family during the Holidays.

Their next performance is within a few weeks, on January 15th for Martin Luther King's birthday. They have enough songs in their repertoire to do this concert. They will rehearse on Thursday and Saturday and o sound check on Sunday evening at 1:00. Brenna is always thinking a head as she is the manager for them and also Terrence. Kevin will be with the group because of Alice's upcoming birth. Kevin will be performing for the ML Holiday as well and Brenna wants to have him booked for that event in case the girls cannot keep that date because of early labor. Brenna is trying to be optimistic about this because they are caring twins and feeling fine right now. This doesn't mean that it will continue to be the case for the two of them. Alice is having her baby sometime in February and won't be able to perform with shekinah Praise for MLK (Martin Luther King's) birthday.

On Wednesday the Snow's, Julie's in-laws will travel back to Syracuse, New York. Brenna and Julie both were kind of quiet and just kind of sitting around and listening to everyone else talking. They spoke softly to each other about how tired they were and just needed to sleep for a few days. Then they discussed the birth of their babies whether they would be ready to go back on tour in May. Both their parents had promised them that they would take care of the babies along with a nanny until the babies are ready for Pre-School. They promised them that they would even travel with the girls because they wanted to breast feed their babies. Julie and Brenna continued their personal conversation until someone ask them if they were being anti-social and they laughed and replied that they were just having a quiet conversation about their little ones. The girls had perked up a little especially when they talked about their babies.

Well the Holidays, Christmas and New Years are behind them and everyone has returned to their homes. It's in the second week of

January and Monday the 16th is Martin Luther King's Holiday. They have three months or less before their babies are born. Twins can arrive earlier than anticipated.

They are now in the studio preparing for the one-day concert for MLK Day. They are only rehearsing on the 11th and the 13th, Wednesday and Friday. Alice is taking the month off because her due date is February. The time has gone by fast and Brenna will not let her perform any more until after she delivers her baby. Brenna is very strict with her safety rules and want their friend to be safe for the baby's sake.

Kevin Snow and Shekinah Praise is all hyped up for this concert. All of their school friends and family shows up for this concert and it is always a blessing just to do this concert for the city. Shekinah Praise knows the songs that they will be performing and this makes it much easier for them to get through the concert. The seven songs will be presented along with a Short skit for the audience. Everything has been put together very nicely according to the program. The church will do the skit and Shekinah Praise along with Kevin Snow will be performing.

Shekinah Praise and Kevin Snow has planned an hour for refreshments and coffee/tea or juice for everyone. They will have the Mayor and Freeholders of the county speak to the kids as well.

Now it is Martin Luther King's birthday and day of the concert. The concert starts at 1:00 PM and everyone is in place and the theatre is packed. The Mayor comes out and speak to the audience about Martin Luther King and then the Freeholders speak after him. Kevin Snow came on first and he did an awesome job with his new song from his new CD. The church group performed their skit to perfection for the children, and right after, Shekinah Praise sang three songs and Kevin Snow joins them and they just performed until everyone in the Theatre was on their feet clapping and singing along with them. They spent an hour and forty- five minutes with their audiences and had time to make sure all the children had refreshments and time to ask questions if they wanted to. What a great and enjoyable time they had during this concert.

The City was so proud of Shekinah Praise and Kevin Snow and

wanted to reschedule them for the following year. They would not commit to this date but they promised the city by the third quarter of the year they would have a firm answer for them. Because of Maternity leaves for the three girls, Alice, Julie and Brenna, they did not want to get themselves into a contract that they can't get out of because they will be dealing with five little precious ones that need nanny's and their mothers to take care of them. They won't make commitments just yet until the girls get or have caregivers in place for their babies. Brenna's mom wants to take care of the babies, but this is an awful lot to put on her mother. She wants the babies to travel with them so they can breast feed the twins unless they are on short trips where they will be back in town on the same day. Brenna and Julie want nannies for a few months to travel with them if they are on tour for a month or so. This will give their mom's some rest as well to do the things they want to do. Julie and Brenna's mom has agreed to travel with them even with the nanny's because they want to make sure their grandbabies are being well taken care of. Brenna says we definitely want our babies with us. I know I want to be near my twins every day and Julie chimed in and said me too.

CHAPTER
TEN

The Deliveries

Alice's baby girl was born February 23rd weighing in at 7 lbs., 12 Oz's. Alice and Terrence named her Alyssa Simone. Terrence and Alice are proud parents of their new daughter and she will also be touring with both of their children. She has her nanny already on board along with both her mom and Terrence's mother. They will alternate between the two of them in helping Alice and Terrence. Their little baby girl is a mixture of Terrence and Alice. Little Alyssa is already a month and a half old now.

Brenna is on complete bed rest and miserable. Julie is still walking around a little but need to be on bed rest as well. After two weeks of bed rest Brenna calls Julie to let her know that her back is really hurting and she is calling her OBGYN to see if she needs to go to the hospital. It is starting the second week of April now and it's time for the twins to make their entrance into James and Brenna's family. After Brenna spoke to her doctor, he wants her to check into the hospital immediately. She already has her bag packed for the two little ones. James is a nervous wreck but manages to get the bag and Brenna into the car. James gets Brenna to the emergency room and parks his car and runs back to Brenna's side and her water had broken and they took her into the delivery room right away. She had been in labor all day but didn't know it. Right after she gets into the delivery room James only had enough time to get into his scrubs before Brenna delivers a baby boy weighing in at 7 lbs. 5 Oz's. James named his son James Myron and five minutes later Brenna delivers a baby girl weighing in at 7 Lbs. 2 Oz's., they named her Jasmine Milan'. Julie was right there with Brenna and, an hour later her water broke while she was in the hospital room with Brenna. She was discreet and went out the room without raising suspicious to Brenna. Thank God they both have the same OBGYN. Julie did not tell Brenna that she thought she was in labor as well but she brought her suitcase along because she felt that she would be staying too. She did not tell Brenna because she did not want to upset her. Brenna was so out of it she went to sleep the minute Julie walked out of the room. Kevin knew Julie was in labor and had told James, that Julie would be delivering that same day. She called Brenna to let her know that she was going home to go to bed. She went to the nurse's station where her doctor was waiting on her to take her to the delivery room. She delivered her daughter Kamryn Renee and five minutes later she delivered her son Kevin Josiah. They weighed in at 6 lbs. 14 Oz's. And 6 lbs. 12 Oz's. All babies and moms are doing fine. Kevin goes into Brenna's room to give her the good news. Brenna kind of knew because Julie was not looking right but was really ready to leave in such a hurry. They put them in rooms next to each other. They were very happy and their husbands were overjoyed that their babies were born on the same day April 12th, the six of us was in the hospital for a week. The boys had to be circumcised and stay in the hospital until they weren't running a fever. When the week was up mothers and babies went home. Brenna was absolutely surprised to see the baby's room so beautiful. Her mom, husband and sisters did a great job in putting the beds together with all their coverings on each bed with two dressing tables attached to each bed. Now the fun begins. Brenna is breast feeding every two hours. Both babies are being fed at the same time she didn't know if she was going to have enough milk for the two of them. The Doctor gave her formula so if she didn't have enough milk for the two of them, she would have formula for them. This is Brenna's first night at home with the twins and her husband. The babies wake up every two hours for feedings. Brenna was able to handle the first three feedings ok with

James help. James is so good with helping her. Sometime she would feed them at the same time and he would just sit and watch her. Sometime she would feed one of the babies while the other one slept and feed the other one later on. Periodically they did not always wake up at the same time, this was a help to Brenna. She started to learn that she needed to pump ahead of time and put into bottles for the next feeding so James could help her. He was just an amazing husband and dad. He sleeps when they are down for the count.

Brenna tells her mom that the babies' looks just like James. They are identical twins. Her mom thinks that they look more like Brenna when she was a baby. She went and retrieved Brenna's baby's pictures and they are exactly like her baby pictures. They already like to be held and they are getting spoiled right now. James loves holding both of them at the same time. Brenna sees him holding and cuddling them all the time. He placed a cot in the baby's room so he can be near them when they wake up. They are beautiful babies with silky straight hair and beautiful grey green eyes. Brenna's mom loves helping her and so does her father. Julie mom and Kevin are doing the same for her. Kevin stays in the baby's room until they are sleep. He and James are making sure their wives are getting enough sleep because near the end of their pregnancy neither one of them was sleeping at all.

Julie and Kevin are enjoying their babies as well. Her husband Kevin really was great as well with feeding the twins in the late-night hours. Kevin and Julie both try to get an hour here and there when the babies are down.

The girls Brenna and Julie got through the first two weeks ok and then it became a routine for them. Their moms were over during the day and this was a great help. They hired two nannies to come in for four hours a day so the babies could get use to them.

The girls, Brenna, Julie and Alice will be returning to the group the end of June. Their tour starts in August and they will be on tour for six to eight weeks with nanny's and their moms in tow. Brenna and Julie spend an hour in the mornings and an hour in the evening planning for their upcoming tour in August with Shekinah Praise and Kevin Snow. Kevin will b be in Syracuse, New York, and New York City later on for a concert. Julie is excited because she gets to spend some time with her in-laws with the twins. They haven't had a lot of time to spend with the twins since they were born because they live in Atlanta and her in-laws live in Syracuse, New York. Mrs. Snow has plans to travel to sites they will be performing at. Julie says she will love this when her mother-in-law shows up. This will be extra special because she has the twins on tour with them. She and Brenna are elated with the babies. Both sets of twins as well as Alice and Terrence's baby girl are growing and starting to recognize their parents and reaching out to them. They are very friendly babies with everyone but they know who their parents are. The five babies are so good with each other. They are like sisters and brothers and are at the cutest stages along with Alice's baby. Brenna, Julie and Alice keep them together so much, so when they grow up, they will be the best of friends like they are. It is now the end of June and Shekinah Praise is getting ready to go on tour. Alice and Terrence baby daughter Alissa Simone are adorable and a month and a few days older than the twins. She is a mixture of both Alice and Terrence. They are so proud of her and little "Terrence Jr., as well. Brenna and James twins are a mixture of both of them. Myron James looks like his dad with eyes and mouth like Brenna. Jasmine Milan looks so much like Brenna, but eyes and nose like James. This is Brenna and James thoughts. The babies are identical twins and so adorable. Brenna knows that it's getting near the time they start preparing for their upcoming tour in New York, New Jersey, Connecticut, Boston, Pennsylvania and Washington, DC. They have been to the studio three times this week rehearsing songs for their tour from their new CD as well as other songs from their repertoire. They will be fully prepared for this tour. They have been together so much and have been going over all their songs so they are really ready to go now. SHEKINAH PRAISE will do a concert at Rev. Snow's church for Kevin's father. They are already well prepared for this concert. This concert will be a gift back to the community for Kevin since they do it for their Pastor back at home in Atlanta.

Julie is so excited about this concert because she gets to spend time with her in-laws in Syracuse, New York with the twins. Her in-laws will have some time to spoil them. They will be in New York for two weeks and then back to Atlanta to start their tour for three weeks in November.

For the entire month of July Shekinah Praise is rehearsing for their upcoming tour. They rehearse three hours in the morning and four hours in the evening. They keep the babies at the studio so they can nurse them. They have a built-in nursery at the studio with six stations to accommodate all the babies their nannies and their mothers. The three new mothers, Brenna, Julie and Alice are beginning to show signs of fatigue. James knows his wife very well and has asked her to take some time to rest. He calls Kevin and Terrence and tells them the girls need a couple of days to rest without any rehearsals. So, they get a reprieve from rehearsals. They spend two hours in the morning and two hours in the afternoon to spend with the babies. The girls rested for twenty-four hours and then it's back to rehearsal again for them. The girls were really happy to spend two whole days with their little ones and get that extra time just to relax and rest with them.

The babies are really growing and learning who their parents really are. Milan' likes to pull on Brenna's hair and lays on James shoulder when she gets upset. Myron just wants all of Brenna's attention and just frets when he is not in Brenna's site. He is a mommy's boy for sure. As long as the other babies are around him, he is happy and plays. He really is a good baby as long as he sees his mom or dad occasionally.

SHEKINAH PRAISE and Kevin Snow, the Artist are scheduled to leave late spring for their up-coming tour on the East Coast and New England area. They are really excited about this tour because they will be showcasing their new CD. Shekinah Praise and Kevin the Artist as well as the rest of the groups were so prepared to show case their New CD and that they certainly are prepared to do. There first stop is Buffalo, Niagara Falls, Rochester and then on to Kevin's home town of Syracuse, NY, late summer. With each show being amazing. Shekinah Praise's concert there in Buffalo was one of their best. They brought the house down in each city after that. Brenna, Julie, and Alice along with their nannies and parents got checked and settled into their hotel rooms in Syracuse. They had their sound check early Saturday morning at 10:00 AM for their 7:00 evening concert. The concert there was amazing and they really put on a show there. The concert was well put together and executed on time. Kevin Snow the Artist was fantastic and he performed like it was his last show. His family was so happy for him and it was home for him. Shekinah Praise stepped out and did the same thing because they knew they had to prove a point in Syracuse. They show cased their new CD in Buffalo and that went over very well. Kevin's father gave them their first break and they wanted Rev. Snow to see that he will never be forgotten for putting them on the map. One of their surprises is an up and coming group that is traveling with them that Brenna and Julie have put together and they are really great. They are basically R&B and Hip Hop but they can put on a great gospel show as well with them. When they are not in the church, they will perform some of their secular hits which they love to do. Brenna's sister is starting her career as a soloist and she performed two songs and that went over great with their audience. Afterward they sold out all of their Tees, pictures and CD's that they had with them. They received every day their CD's, pictures and tees to be sold to their audience.

Back at the hotel they were so overwhelmed and over joyed that they couldn't sleep. But reality sunk in real soon fast when the babies awaken and wanted to be changed and fed. They played for about twenty minutes and fell fast asleep. The nannies took the babies and made sure they were ready for bed again.

Brenna wanted to go to bed for some relaxation and rest. After cuddling with her husband, she reminded him that they needed to get rest for the concert on Saturday evening. Sound check was at 11:00 AM for four hours or less. They had gotten a goodnight sleep and was up at 9:00 AM to take care of their little ones and then on to sound check. It only took them two hours forty-five minutes as the sound system was superb and when their music is on point, they can do what is needed to be done. They have great engineers with them that take care of their music where ever they go. They returned back to their hotel and fed the babies and made sure they were fully hydrated and ate something themselves as well. Afterward Brenna pumped milk for the little ones and then they showered and dressed for their trip to their next concert. They made it to their dressing room with their attire. They changed in the dressing room for the concert. The concert was amazing with everyone being on point. The music was set at the right tone and all went well. Brenna was totally on a spiritual high and James stepped up and both brought the house down. The concert in Buffalo, Niagara Falls, Rochester, Syracuse, NY City and Long Island all were great. They were tired but they took a couple of days off when they got into Hartford, CT. This concert was awesome as well. They did the tour in Connecticut, Hartford, New Haven, Waterbury and Danbury. When Shekinah Praise and Kevin Snow finished up the tour in Connecticut, they traveled to New Jersey where they did the same concert in Newark, Jersey City, Plainfield, Camden and Trenton. Shekinah Praise, Kevin Snow and the rest of the tour moved on to Philadelphia, PA and then into Baltimore Maryland. The tour ended in the nation's capital of Washington, DC. Shekinah Praise and Kevin Snow tour got such rave reviews as they completed their last week in Washington DC. They will be resting for two to three weeks and maybe a Christmas concert at their hometown of Atlanta, GA. Brenna has not booked Atlanta yet because they always work on a concert for their home church to give back to the community. Shekinah Praise never forget where they came from and always work with Pastor Derrick for the Holidays. This concert will always be free to the community because Pastor Derrick grew up with them and they have such a great admiration and connection for and to him as their career originated in his church. He let them use the church to put their songs together to rehearse and just do whatever they had to do to get the group set up and into the studios. He will always be an integral part of their life and their group.

Kevin Snow and Shekinah Praise have been so busy that they cannot keep up with the time or days anymore. Brenna and Julie planned the Christmas concert for Pastor Derrick to be held four days before Christmas and everything was so organized that the concert went off without any problems or concerns even down to the decorations which was simply beautiful and amazing. Pastor Derrick wanted to know where they get the talent and the time to do such beautiful work of art. Brenna laughed and said skilled training from home and school. Julie chimed in and said if you were raised in our homes you knew how to do everything. Pastor Derrick said well noted.

Brenna and James started the concert off with Christmas carols and then into their Christmas songs. Julie and Kevin came on and sang their version of their Christmas songs. Shekinah Praise joined in with Kevin Snow, and the rest of the church as they went through their songs. Alice did her new song with Terrence and the entire Shekinah Praise group. They left everything out on the floor. Franklin spoke briefly and almost preached before he sang his song. And when he speaks everyone listen and then he sings. What an awesome blessing coming from him. He is the only ordained preacher in Shekinah Praise. Franklin is a worship leader and dynamite preacher. He does it all, preaches and sings as well. He is never lost for words when it comes to our Lord and Savior Jesus Christ. He knows the Bible. His performance was fantastic and then we brought our new group on that we are grooming and introduced them to Pastor Derrick and his congregation. They are performing with us for the Holidays and they are great already. Brenna gets the MIC and let the audience know that We praise God for our new group and we know they will be recording sometime in the future and we are so looking forward to working with them. Although they are R & B Singers that know the Lord as we do, we are equally as proud of them too. They wanted to show case their talent here in Atlanta, so what better way to do that than do it in the House of the Lord. God said as long as you keep him first and center in your life you will go farther in life. Praise God and did everyone have a great time here tonight. Did you enjoy the concert? Well we are doing this last song that I think everyone knows or can follow along with us. "Mary did you Know". They finished this song and the church was on another spiritual high and it took some time for the church to calm down. The Christmas program ended around the 11:00 hour, just fantastic.

They sold out of their CD's and all other items on sale for Shekinah Praise that night at the church. The donations from the church for service went to the church but the CD's and other items were profits for Shekinah Praise. The church was given a gift of two hundred fifty CD's to be sold by the church for their profit. Pastor Derrick was beyond words with this gift. They had this packaged from their recordings and put in a gift bag to the Church from Shekinah Praise to be for the soul purpose of the church. This was a write off for the group because Pastor Derrick has been so good to them and they will do anything for him and the church because of the way he treated them. Shekinah Praise also promised to have some of their new CD's within six months to give to Pastor as well.

Now everyone is off to their respective homes for the holidays to celebrate Christmas. Brenna and James are sort of tired and made sure the babies are fed for the night and the Nanny stayed over to take care of the little ones. This is the babies first Christmas and they don't know quite what it's all about yet but we're sure they will love playing with their little fluffy toys and gadgets. They are just adorable and James and Kevin are loving every minute of it. We'll have all five babies together and Terrence and Alice's two-year-old son on Christmas night and they are just having a blast. We are expecting our parents to come to our home for a great celebration between all the families of Shekinah Praise and friends on Christmas Eve. We know our home will be such a welcoming of all their friends and family. Everyone came over and gifts were exchanged between Shekinah Praise and then on to the families. Our parents did a great job of selecting gifts for all who attended and even bought extra in case someone else showed up unexpected. It was a grand party and around 4:00 AM it was time that everyone decided to find their respected homes.

Everyone goes home and Brenna and James stay at her mom's home because the twins were put down in the nursery her mom had prepared at her home and they did not want to leave them. Early on Christmas morning they took them home so they can get a look at their Christmas tree and play with their stuffed animals. James and I took pictures of them with different animals and watched them play with them and had fun taking pictures. Kevin and Julie did the same as they are practically next door to James and Brenna and they came over for an hour to let the little ones play together. They are doing a concert on New Year's Eve and then they are going to take some time off to be with their family for a while. Brenna told the entire group that they will be on leave until after all the babies are born. They all need some rest and relaxation. Brenna has already discussed with the new group that they will be doing the MLK concert and she will be working with them because they are new to the business and need to continue traveling and recording. Terrence, Rodney, James brother will be the manager for them when the new group is on the road. Brenna and Julie are handling the recording and the bookings for the new Artist. "They will not be traveling with them until after the babies are a year old.

Well the Holidays are over and Shekinah Praise will take a Sabbatical for six months. They will work on recordings rentals of the studio and other projects to keep the business financially stable.

Franklin has given us updates on his wife Arianna's pregnancy. Their baby will be born in May and Johnny and Camille will have their baby in July. Everyone is so excited

The babies are growing so fast and they will be a year old after the New Year. The year has really gone so fast and Brenna, Julie, Alice and their husbands are wondering where the time has gone. Johnny, Camille, Arianna and Franklin and the rest of the group are on a hiatus for a few weeks of rest and relaxation. All of the members of the group have gotten married now and just having fun in the Lord and singing his praises throughout the Atlanta Area. No out of state bookings until after the six months leave.

Now that they have their own recording Studio, they can do all of their work without hiring outside people to come in and do the recording. Within their group is musical engineers and people that do the sound system all within their family. They are a great musical family that can handle their own recordings and anything else within the musical field. They realized this while they were all in college and decided to get degrees in what they needed for a recording studio. They have their own band within the family. Everyone plays an instrument or drums, whatever they need is in the family.

As Brenna Smaller sat in her home now reminiscing about how she and her best friend Julie Glass who were eleven years old at the time met and became best friends and how they met two cousins and really had crushes on them. Brenna had a crush on James Williams and Julie had a crush on Johnny Williams. As Brenna got a few years older, falling in love with James Williams was the highlight of her life but she had to love this young man from a distance because they were very young and her parents did not let her date until she was fifteen years old. When she could date James, they were totally inseparable with a few bumps in the road in high school, and into college for four years and still dated.

This was really true love as Brenna did love him from a distance and then within the distance of life in college. Both of the girls had great love interest that blossomed into engagement, NOW MARRIAGE and families.

Printed in the United States
By Bookmasters